# The Rhetorical Short Story

*Best American Short Stories on War and
the Military, 1915–2006*

**William M. Purcell**

I0592433

University Press of America,® Inc.
Lanham · Boulder · New York · Toronto · Plymouth, UK

**Copyright © 2009 by**
**University Press of America,® Inc.**
4501 Forbes Boulevard
Suite 200
Lanham, Maryland 20706
UPA Acquisitions Department (301) 459-3366

Estover Road
Plymouth PL6 7PY
United Kingdom

Library of Congress Control Number: 2009934345
ISBN-13: 978-0-7618-4869-1 (clothbound : alk. paper)
ISBN-10: 0-7618-4869-X (clothbound : alk. paper)
ISBN-13: 978-0-7618-4870-7 (paperback : alk. paper)
ISBN-10: 0-7618-4870-3 (paperback : alk. paper)
eISBN-13: 978-0-7618-4871-4
eISBN-10: 0-7618-4871-1

♾™The paper used in this publication meets the minimum
requirements of American National Standard for Information
Sciences—Permanence of Paper for Printed Library Materials,
ANSI Z39.48-1992

This book is dedicated to my late parents, George William Purcell (1925-2004) and Esther Christina Bond Purcell (1927-2004), my wife, Jodie Kathleen Williams Purcell, and to my daughter, Esther Kathleen Purcell. You have all made me what I am and continue to inspire me to what I hope to become.

# Contents

.

# Acknowledgements

A scholarly work is a collaborative product. We all benefit from relationships with teachers, colleagues and students. In particular, I would like to thank the late Eugene Current-Garcia who, over 30 years ago at Auburn University, gave a struggling young man a measure of hope by simply writing "Good job!" on a college essay. To this day I can think of no higher praise. My friends and colleagues, David Snowball, Thomas Tryzna, Kris Freeman, Shannon Scott, and Molly Mayhead, all read portions of this work and provided both criticism and encouragement. Portions of Chapter Two were presented to the Beers Research Roundtable at Seattle Pacific University. Thank you for making the job of writing a little less lonely. I am also thankful to have been facilitated in my research and writing for this project by a sabbatical leave granted by Seattle Pacific University in 2005-06.

I would like to thank the following authors for permission to quote from their works: Benjamin Percy for "Refresh, Refresh," copyright © 2005 by Benjamin Percy. Reprinted by permission of the author and Curtis Brown, Ltd.; John Bart Gerald, "Walking Wounded," copyright © 1968 by John Bart Gerald. Quotations reprinted with permission of the author; John Bart Gerald, "Blood Letting," copyright ©1969 by John Bart Gerald. Quotations reprinted with permission of the author; Thom Jones, "The Pugilist at Rest," copyright ©1991 by Thom Jones. Reprinted by permission of the author; Larry Heinemann, "The First Clean Fact" by Larry Heinemann. Copyright © 1979 by Larry Heinemann. Quoted by permission of the author; .Robert Olen Butler, "Salem" by Robert Olen Butler. Copyright © 2001by Robert Olen Butler. Used by Permission of Grove/Atlantic, Inc.

# Introduction

Since 1915, over 2,100 stories have been published in over 90 annual volumes of *Best American Short Stories*.[1] Contained within those volumes are 2,100 rich snapshots of American life. Writers told of life in small towns, the isolation of rural existence, the toughness of the big city. They wrote of family and community, alienation and isolation. They wrote about blacks and whites, Asians and Indians, Southerners and Yankees. They wrote, poignantly at times, callously at others, of the various tensions between races, religions, and creeds. And they wrote of wars: the Civil War (or, War Between the States), the Great War (later downgraded to World War I), World War II, Korea, Vietnam, and, now, Iraq. The series was founded during the Great War; 22 of its stories comment on that conflict. The series' first editor, Edward J. O'Brien, died in the early days of World War II after selecting the stories for 26 years. The second editor, Martha Foley, began selecting the stories in 1942 and continued until 1977, two years after the final American withdrawal from Vietnam. The stories written in wartime bring out an awareness of America's changing attitudes towards war and the military.

The war stories tell us more about America than its military conflicts, however. The portrayal of war and military service is a unifying theme that captures diverse elements of the American experience. The stories reflect our problems, tensions, and triumphs. Some 92 stories, spanning the Great War to Iraq, provide brief glimpses of an important element of American life, but also the societal forces in play during various military stages. Together, they provide a rich tapestry of the American story, both warp and weft. The tapestry is at the same time realistic and spiritual, mundane and grandiloquent, domestic and foreign. It feels the strain of colors and creeds forced to work in harmony: black, white, yellow; Jewish and Gentile. The design in the tapestry is not always flattering; nor is it particularly intelligent. It is optimistic and pessimistic; real and fanciful; new and old. It is part of our story, written by our fathers and mothers, sisters and brothers, friends and enemies, neighbors and strangers.

Paul Fussell has written two compelling books about the literature of the two world wars of the Twentieth Century: *The Great War and Modern Memory* (1975) and *Wartime: Understanding and Behavior in the Second World War* (1989). Both volumes provide important insights to the nature of war and its myths, realities, lies, and legends. Fussell's works focus primarily on novels and memoirs, but do not discuss short fiction, no doubt for the reason that 2-3,000 short stories are published each year. I hope this study can serve to complement, in a modest way, Fussell's fine contribution. This study is tries to understand the stories by engaging their complexity, ambiguity, and irony. It tries to comprehend the stories in a larger context.

Indeed, it is the various contexts in which the stories were written that tweak my academic curiosity as a rhetorician. I find the war stories most interesting because they have something to say about their time and place. They are rhetorical. In his landmark 1925 essay, "The Literary Criticism of Oratory," Herbert Wichelns drew a bright line between literary criticism and rhetorical criticism when he wrote "[Rhetorical Criticism] is not concerned with permanence, nor yet with beauty. It is concerned with effect. It regards speech as a communication to a specific audience, and holds its business to be the analysis and appreciation of the orator's method of imparting his ideas as to his hearers."[2] The definition proves to be a useful heuristic, as it separates the purviews of rhetorical and literary studies. Indeed, it was not until the publication of Edwin Black's *Rhetorical Criticism: a Study in Method* (1965) that rhetorical consideration of other non-oratorical artifacts began to be countenanced. Black challenged his readers to consider rhetorical phenomena on a broad continuum, with traditional speech and argumentation occupying the center. In the past 40 years the rhetorical lens has scanned a broad variety of rhetorical phenomena: film, television, history, science, romance novels, music, cyberspace, and "visuals."

Consideration of the short story as a rhetorical genre is concerned less with permanence and beauty and more with the analysis of a writer's perceptions presented to a particular audience in a particular time and place. Permanence and beauty, of course, are still a concern, but the brevity of the medium often binds it to time and place. Short stories are also a bit ephemeral. They go out of print quickly and are not as easily available as novels.[3] The rhetorical dimension becomes particularly prominent when a story addresses social issues such as war, peace, and oppression.

When I speak of the idea of the rhetorical short story I take as a point of departure the fact that the inherent brevity of a short story makes it share similarities with a speech or an essay: it can be read/heard/processed in one sitting. This characteristic allows the reader of the short story, unlike the reader of a novel, to experience a sustained, uninterrupted sense of mood. As Edgar Allan Poe wrote, "During the hour of perusal the soul of the reader is at the writer's control. There are no external or extrinsic influences—resulting from weariness or interruption."[4] The main component used in these stories is what I shall call rhetorical depiction. Rhetorical depiction features the creation of word pictures, scenes that connect with the reader to present a feeling that is more powerful than speech. This dimension seems to provide and exploit reactions that the reader, in connection with the writer and reader's shared context, brings to the reading. Some short stories also utilize speech, rather than dialogue, as a means of creating a type of soapbox from which to express their views. Given that a short story can have a much shorter time of composition and publication than a novel; it also can reflect more precisely the evolution and change of a society's attitude toward a particular issue over time.

Mr. O'Brien repeatedly wrote in the prefaces to his volumes that a short story should bear two essential elements: substance and form. By substance, O'Brien meant the writer's ability to transform the basic facts via "the artist's power of compelling imaginative persuasion, transform[ing] them into a living truth." Form was achieved by "shap[ing] this living substance into the most beautiful and satisfying form, by skillful selection and arrangement of his material, and by the most direct and appealing presentation of it in portrayal and characterization."[5] Indeed, O'Brien's focus on form encompasses the first three canons of classical rhetoric: invention, arrangement, and style. His notion of a "living truth" comes very close to rhetorical depiction. Ms. Foley went even farther, suggesting the enthymematic nature of the short story. In 1955 she wrote that, since the advent of printing, the short story "has become like the act of love. It takes place between two people, the writer and reader."[6] She addressed the issue again in 1962. The short story writer differs from all others, she wrote, in that "a short story writer suggests more than his space allows him to say."[7] By lodging the definition of the short story in the completion provided by the audience, Foley places the short story squarely in the rhetorical realm. The successful short story must connect with a particular audience, an audience situated in a place and time. In essence, then, a short story is an enthymeme, a type of rhetorical demonstration that requires the participation of an audience/reader to complete.[8] Indeed, Aristotle included the fable as a means of enthymematic proof. A fable generates a scenario drawn from an existing situation to make a point. It is no wonder, then, that many of the selected stories come across as pretenses for giving speeches. It is also not insignificant that in *The Best American Short Stories of the Century*, a collection of the 56 best stories from the series, selected by John Updike, none of the stories of interest here appears, except for Philip Roth's "Defender of the Faith" (1960) and Tim O'Brien's "The Things They Carried" (1987). Indeed, many of the stories from the Great War appear particularly odd to contemporary readers. Rhetorically successful messages don't always stand the test of time.

O'Brien and Foley were formidable editors who selected the volumes from popular and literary publications in the years spanning 1915 and 1977. O'Brien, who lived in England for the last twenty years of his life, died during the London blitz of February, 1941. Foley then inherited the series from O'Brien and steadfastly shepherded the project until her own death at the age of 80. The founding editors took the selection of the "best" stories with much seriousness. Not only did O'Brien select the "best" stories, he compiled a series of lists that ranked the year's short story output in a "Roll of Honor" that identified stories as distinguished, with tiers of rankings designated by one, two, or three asterisks.[9] Foley continued the "Roll of Honor," but without the asterisks. Since Foley's death, the volumes' selections have been made by yearly "guest editors," ranging from Ted Soltaroff (1978) and John Updike (1984) to Garrison Keillor (1998) and Walter Mosley (2003) with prior screening from "coeditors," Shannon Ravenal (1978-90), Katrina Kennison (1991-2006), and Heidi Pitlor (2007). The contemporary editors are not as confident as O'Brien and Foley in naming the best stories. They are loath to proclaim their selections as "best" and are generally apologetic in making their choices. I understand their reluctance. Nonetheless, both O'Brien and Foley, for good or ill, were resolutely decisive in making their selections. They operated under consistent assumptions as to what constitutes "best." In contrast the selections in the later editions were picked by a different judge each year. In spite of best intentions, standards will vary from editor to editor. As John Edgar Wideman, the editor in 1996, wrote: "Once the protective mark of objectivity is scuttled or scuttles itself, a simple fact remains: the stories in this book are stories I like ."[10]

   *Best American Short Stories* is not the only continuous collection of American short stories. Doubleday has produced an annual collection called the *Prize Stories: The O'Henry Awards* since 1918. I have reviewed the contents of many of the O'Henry collections. They differ markedly from the *Best American Short Stories* in consistency and rhetorical value. Something about the presence of two selectors/editors over the course of 62 years has made the Best volumes more suitable as rhetorical artifacts. Indeed, I had originally planned to end this study at 1977, the final year of Martha Foley's editorship. Because important stories relating to Vietnam appeared in subsequent years, I continued the survey through 2007. Surprisingly, the enlarged time span provided another dimension to World War II (concentration camp narratives), but very little on the American involvement in the Persian Gulf between 1990 and 2007. It is also surprising that none of the selected stories has addressed the events of 11 September 2001 and its aftermath. Indeed, it was only in 2006 that a story mentioned the war in Iraq.

   Generally, the stories in the series were selected from those published in a twelve month period in the year previous to publication. Hence, *Best American Short Stories, 1945* includes stories published chiefly in 1944. [11] The year stated in the title, then, is the year after which the stories were initially published. Accordingly, some stories were often written a year or two before their publication in the series. The founding editors presented their final selections in alphabetical order. The practice of alphabetical listing has, for the most part, been discarded, sometimes to facilitate thematic groupings and at other times for the apparent purpose of randomness.

To twist the title of Wicheln's classic essay, this study addresses the "Oratorical Criticism of Literature." The thesis is that the short story represents a discrete rhetorical genre, particularly evident in stories involving social unrest. The "effect" in a short story is not so much the impact a story has on its readers, but more the impact that the readers, the audience, have on the story itself. The stories reviewed here therefore are receptacles of the spirit and mood of their times. The study proceeds on two levels. First, it follows the war and military stories published in *Best American Short Stories* as a narrative of American social history from 1915 to 2004. Second, it considers the short story as a rhetorical genre by examining the way in which the stories function as enthymemes in their particular socio-historical contexts. Kenneth Burke's dramatistic pentad, provides a helpful perspective for examining the motives expressed in rhetorical documents. According to Burke, a way to attribute motives in a communicative act is to regard that act as a drama consisting of Act, Scene, Agent, Agency, and Purpose. Each element of the pentad asks a particular question about the communicative occurrence: a focus on act asks what was done; an emphasis on scene asks when or where the act was committed; scrutiny on the agent addresses who performed the act; a concern with agency addresses how the act was performed; a concern with purpose asks why the act was committed.[12] Burke further aligns the elements of the pentad with particular philosophies: scene-materialism, agent-idealism, agency-pragmatism, purpose-mysticism, act-realism.[13] Hence, a message with a predominant focus on purpose would reveal a mystical motive, while one bearing a primary emphasis on the agent would reveal an idealist intent. A focus on scene indicates a materialist view. That emphasis, he posits, gives rise to what he regards as a type of objective, scientific analysis which, in spite of its arbitrariness, leads one to assume the presence of inherent, material drives toward certain behavior.[14] An act is therefore portrayed as the inevitable consequence of its scene, or material conditions. We will find that the rhetorical depiction in these stories fluctuates drastically over time, from a view that emphasizes the purpose in a story, often in relation to agents, to one that emphasizes the scene in which the story is told. By focusing on the implied completions provided by the readers of the story I hope to provide a more fulsome account of the times in which they were written.

The account begins with the early days of World War I, prior to the United States' entry in 1917, when writers portrayed a strange and distant European war, while still clinging to romantic memories of the Civil War. With the United States' entrance into the fray in 1917, the tone of the stories changes to one more concerned with bolstering the war effort. In mid-war the accounts begin to feature spiritual and supernatural themes, including ghosts and angels, aimed at finding a reason to justify the war's carnage. Finally, some ten years after the war's end in 1918, the accounts begin to take on a realistic tone.

The coming of the second war is chronicled well before the United States' involvement, in a series of stories beginning in 1937. As in the first war the early accounts portray the European struggles from the perspective of outsiders. With the arrival in America of refugees from Europe in the late thirties and early forties, however, the stories become much more involved.

A domestic focus, essentially absent from most stories about the Great War, is a strong presence in the stories of World War II. Only a few stories about that conflict feature accounts of combat. Most focus on the home front, or on soldiers away from the battlefield. Although there is no stated opposition to the war in the stories of that period, the unstated conclusion that connects with reader is that the war is certainly unwelcome. Unlike the first war, these stories feature very few accounts of spirituality. The realistic tone continues.

The post-war stories move in a variety of directions. Interestingly, they carry a heightened awareness of racial and ethnic tensions which, in most cases, are depicted in training camp settings. The stories of Vietnam, somewhat like World War I, are quite explicit. Unlike World War I, they are starkly realistic. Two post-Vietnam stories, "Salem" and "The Pugilist at Rest," return in mild form to the spiritual tenor of World War I. They provide an interesting element of closure for the twentieth century. The final story considered, one relating to the Iraq War, invites a startling comparison with some early stories of the Great War.

# Endnotes

1. The series ran under the title of *Best Short Stories 1915 and the Yearbook of the American Short Story* and continued with that title, with the year changed, until 1942. In 1942 the series was known as *Best American Short Stories, 1942, and Yearbook of the American Short Story*. In 1978 the title was revised to *Best American Short Stories, 1978, Selected from U. S. and Canadian Magazines, including the Yearbook of the American Short Story*. The clause "including the Yearbook of the American Short Story" was dropped in 1982. The title has remained the same since that time.

2. Herbert Augustus Wichelns, "The Literary Criticism of Oratory," in *Studies in Rhetoric and Public Speaking in Honor of James Albert Winans by Pupils and Colleagues* (New York: The Century Company, 1925), 209.

3. Libraries do not routinely maintain back copies of *Best American Short Stories*. I had great difficulty in obtaining a complete set of volumes needed for this study. Ultimately, I purchased around 70 copies from booksellers with sites on the worldwide web. Many of the volumes I purchased were former library copies from public and university libraries across the United States, including the University of Iowa (1931, 1935, 1938, 1940), Brooklyn, NY (1980), Renton, WA (1933), Seymour, IN (1934), Elgin Air Force Base (1978, 1981), Hillsboro, OR (1979), Worthington, OH (1939), Ft. Benjamin Harrison, IN (1941), The Elks National Home, Fairfax, VA (1967), Richland County, SC (1982), Dayton and Montgomery Counties, OH (1978), and Jennings County, IN (1974).

4. Poe 8.

5. Edward J. O'Brien, ed., *The Best Short Stories of 1915 and the Yearbook of the American Short Story* (Boston: Small, Maynard and Company, 1916) 7.

6. Martha Foley, ed. *Best American Short Stories, 1955, and Yearbook of the American Short Story* (Boston: Houghton Mifflin, 1955) x.

7. Foley, in Foley, Martha and David Burnett, eds. *Best American Short Stories, 1962, and Yearbook of the American Short Story* (New York: Ballantine, 1962. 1962) vii.

8. Aristotle, *Aristotle on Rhetoric: A Theory of Civic Discourse; Newly Translated with Introduction, Notes, and Appendixes by George A. Kennedy.* (Oxford: Oxford University Press, 1991), 40, 186-90; Bitzer Lloyd, "Aristotle's Enthymeme Revisited," *Quarterly Journal of Speech* 45 (1959): 408.

9. Jacquelyn S. Spangler has argued that O'Brien, who aimed to improve the status of the short story, ultimately made the genre less popular, and created an American literary aesthetic that excluded stories by women, immigrants, and persons of color. See her Edward J. O'Brien: *Best Short Stories* and the Production of an American Genre, unpublished diss., Ohio State University, 1997.

10. John Edgar Wideman, ed., *The Best American Short Stories Selected from U. S, and Canadian Magazines, 1996* (Boston: Houghton Mifflin, 1996) xvi.

11. The time span varies in the early years. For example, most of the stories in the 1915 volume were published in 1915.

12. Kenneth Burke, *A Grammar of Motives* (1945; Berkeley, CA: University of California Press, 1969 xv.

13. Burke 138.
14. Burke 49.

# Chapter One
# The Great War:
# Slaughter, Spirits, and the Facts

The stories about the Great War were written amidst a rapidly changing context. The isolationist America of 1914-16 tended to view the war as a peculiarly European malady. American writers at the time portrayed the war in Europe in ironic terms that highlighted the slaughter, but distanced themselves from the conflict. While the Europeans were killing each other with horrible modern weapons—airplanes, tanks, machine guns, gas, and chemicals— American writers also continued to spin tales about the American Civil War, which had taken place 50 years before. Filmmaker D. W. Griffith's now notorious "Birth of a Nation" came out in 1915. Griffith followed "Birth of the Nation" the next year with his antiwar epic, "Intolerance." One of the more popular songs of 1915-16 was "I Didn't Raise My Boy to Be a Soldier." Woodrow Wilson ran for reelection in 1916 with the slogan: "He kept us out of war." By 1917, however, it was evident that America would soon need to enter the conflict. Popular songs embraced the war with titles such as "Goodbye Broadway, Hello France" and "Over There."

Short story writers responded to the United States entry into the war in two interrelated ways. The first was to cast the carnage of the war as being in accord with some higher purpose. Stories were written with a spiritual overlay that serves to justify participation in the horrible war. A means of resolving the entry into the madness seemed to be a supernatural, or spiritual one—the only "logical" reason to enter the debacle. Two writers worked at reviving American myths of the previous centuries with a patriotic spirituality to help urge young men into action. At the war's end, questions about the war's purpose remained, and some writers engaged in retrospective attempts to make sense of it, again from a spiritual realm. A final phase that does not appear until nearly ten years after the war moves to a realistic portrayal and treats some of the less honorable aspects of the war. An interesting thread that continues up to the current day features stories about the American Civil war, remembered in a fond, romantic fashion.

Perhaps the most distinctive aspect of the stories from the Great War involves the narration. With few exceptions, the stories involve a narrator, a story teller, who presents the stories in a particularly oral fashion. Often cast as second hand accounts, the stories draw veracity from absent others as they tend to sermonize on the events at hand. The stories often feature a long explanation in speech in which the intent of the writer is given voice. The mode is more of a story being told rather than written. By the World War II era, however, the mode is the more omniscient one of a writer.

The first volume of *Best Short Stories*, in 1915, features four stories which address the Great War, already in its full, frustrating fury. While the Great War escalates in Europe, however, American writers are also memorializing the Civil War. Elsie Singmaster wrote two stories of reconciliation that appear in 1915 and 1916 that provide a revealing contrast to the stories coming from the war in Europe. "The Survivors: A Memorial Day Story" (*The Outlook*, 26 May 1915), is set in the border town of Fosterville. All of Fosterville's young men, save one, Adam Foust, had served with the Union army. Adam, whose mother was a southerner, served with the Confederates. Adam returns home on the morning of the first Memorial Day, in 1868. Appalled by the parade of colors and uniforms he still counted as his enemy, Adam donned his Confederate uniform later that day and marched, solo, from one end of the town to the other. The act alienated him from friends and family, including his beloved cousin, Henry, with whom he had been raised. For the next 40 years he continued his solitary yearly march, as well as occasional lone parades in front of the G. A. R. (Grand Army of the Republic) hall during meetings. Townspeople urged him to forget the war and to reunite with his friends and family. Adam steadfastly refused, replying: "Those G. A. R. fellows don't forget it . . . they haven't changed their principles. Why should I change mine?"[1] When urged to reunite with his cousin, Henry, who is becoming the town's leading and wealthiest citizen, Adam refuses, but allows that he would help Henry if he ever needed him.

By the fortieth anniversary of Memorial Day, only Henry was physically able to march for the G. A. R. Adam looked on, clad as usual, in his Confederate gray. Seeing his cousin looking pale and faltering in step, Adam burst forcefully through the crowd to aid his ailing cousin. Marshals rode out to restrain Adam as he called out: "Henry, do you want me to walk along?"[2] Henry looked over to his cousin's tearful eyes and dismissed the marshals. Adam speaks: "I saw you were alone. . . . I said, 'Henry needs me.' I know what it is to be alone." Henry replies: "Of course I need you! . . . I've needed you all along."[3]

Singmaster's romantic view of the war and division was followed the next year by a second story, "Penance" (*Pictorial Review*, October, 1916) written in a somewhat allegorical tone. This story features a young Confederate officer, Buckingham, who has endured four long years of war and, though only 26, is a war-weary general. He no longer has illusions about success in the war: "With clear eyes he foresees the long future of poverty and homelessness. All the possessions of the family, even the last of his mother's trinkets, had gone into the bottomless treasury of the Great Cause and his house had been laid in ashes."[4] Once again he was to lead his division to the site of another battle. Buckingham was distracted, however. His mind drifted back to a pre-war trip to Italy. He attends a staff meeting where he receives his orders for the next morning's battle and is escorted to a millhouse which has been commandeered to house him for the night. He was met coldly by a stout woman, sheltering a small boy behind her skirts. The woman sends a beautiful young woman, named Minnie, to show him to his room. He sleeps well that night, dreaming of the beautiful young woman. The next morning he goes to the table, where, he is told, the young woman will serve him breakfast. After serving him a very leisurely breakfast, the young woman tempts Buckingham with a kiss and he responds most eagerly. The consequence of his brief interlude is that his division is late for the battle and was routed in the final skirmish of the "Great Cause."[5]

Buckingham survives the battle, unscathed, but is consumed with guilt over his blunder. He returns to his family home, takes up residence in the former overseer's cottage and works hard for many years to restore the plantation to working order. Secretly, he sends most of his income to the wives and children of the men killed in that final battle. For years he keeps a loaded pistol with him as a possible cure, should his shame become too much to bear. He dreams repeatedly of Minnie, but refrains from returning to the scene of his shameful last battle.

Some thirty years pass and, at the request of the government, he returns to the battlefield to assist in marking the details of that fateful event. A tour guide takes Buckingham to the scene of his disgrace, unaware of his identity. The guide tells him a story. The guide, it turns out, was the young boy sheltered by his mother the night before the battle. He tells Buckingham that, unknown to history, his mother and cousin had conspired to delay the general from a timely departure for the battle. Upon reaching the battle site, Buckingham dismisses the guide. He stands at the scene, silently reading the markers. He remembers the day and those who died there: "Then suddenly he lifted his head and laid his hands across his breast. "Now,' said he thickly. 'I am free. I have done penance enough.'"[6]

Though clearly stories of reconciliation, both of Singmaster's stories feature extended periods of penance and alienation endured by former Confederate soldiers. The bitterness both protagonists hold contains very little reference to the war itself, but rather, to aspects of their personal character. Each man is portrayed as a tragic, but heroic figure. Stories of the American Civil War appear periodically, up to 2004, yet always with a sense of romantic heroism. This type of portrayal will contrast sharply with most of the stories pertaining to twentieth century wars. The Civil war themes define something of a watermark for a simpler time in America. The survivors are heroic men, whose character is defined by their eventual acts of reconciliation rather than by the war in which they fought. This contrasts with the stories of the Great War which portray an arena in which thoughts of reconciliation are unthinkable amidst the senseless slaughter.

# Senseless Slaughter

Early in the war the stories portray scenes of a bizarre, European war in which any conception of normalcy has gone awry. Will Levington Comfort's "Chautonville" (*The Masses*, August, 1915) takes place on the Eastern front, in the trenches between Russian and Austrian troops. Though relatively early in the war, the malaise had already set in, as expressed in the voice of the first person narrator: "They said that the Russian line was 100 miles long. I know nothing about that, but I know that it extended as far as the eye could reach to the east and west, and that this had been so for many weeks. But *time*, as it is noted in the outer world, had stopped for us. It was now November, and we had been without mails since late in August."[7] Though certainly a long time in 1914, the scene hardly compares to the tedium that four more years of the actual war would bring.

Russian officers, desperate in their attempts to break through the Austrian lines, had enlisted the aid of Chautonville, a celebrated singer of Russian folk songs, to rally the troops for a decisive surge to overwhelm Austrian forces. The narrator, an enlisted man working in headquarters, is appalled by the ploy and privately vows that someday he will "get" the singer. Our narrator is chosen to escort Chautonville to the "pits," which, he describes heroically in periodic style:

> stretched out in either direction—bitten into the ground by the most miserable men the light of day uncovered. I heard their voices—men of my own country—voices as from swooning men—lost to all mercy, ready to die, not as men, but preying, cornered animals, forgotten of God, it seemed, though that was illusion; forgotten of home, which was worse to their hearts, and illusion, too. For we could not hold the facts of home ... only death seemed sure.[8]

Chautonville's manner in approaching the troops, however, is not the contrived, cynical approach the narrator expects. The genuineness of his song transforms the troops. No longer devastated by the grim reality of war, Chautonville created a situation that was "like sitting by a fire, and falling into a dream." The narrator now progresses into a powerful peroration, again in periodic style, heightening the emotion of the moment through the use of repetition: Chautonville "sang of fathers and our boyhood," "Sang of savory kitchens and red fire-lit windows," "sang of ice breaking in rivers," "sang of churches." Soon, the troops "were roaring like schoolboys now behind him." The soldiers no longer rushed into battle, but into a vision of home: "And each of us saw *our* fields, our low earth-thatched barns, and each of us saw our mothers, and every man's father sang." Chautonville sang with the "voice of an angel." "[H]e was singing us home."[9] Chautonville's voice assumed Godlike qualities: "That his voice came through to us—not in the great dusky baritone of song, but like the command of the Father: '*Come on, men, we are going home!*'"

The men have a mystical response to the song. The narrator, felled by a pistol, watches enviously:

All who heard the singing turned homeward. And the lines came in from the east and from the west and deluged them. Propped on my elbow, I saw them go down in the deluge of the obedient—watched until the blood went out and blurred the picture. . . . I wished that I could die with them. It was not slaughter, but martyrdom. It called me through the darkness—and I knew that some man's song would reach all the armies—all men turning home together, each with his vision, and unafraid.[10]

Comfort has captured the senselessness of trench warfare, of warfare in general, and connected with the almost spiritual call of patriotism. This spirituality, in various forms, is a strong motif seen in the stories published throughout the war. This tale, at least in retrospect, strikes something of a cautionary chord: very simple things can be used to urge men to die for their countries.

The uplifting spirituality signaled in "Chautonville" is interspersed by the eerie in W. A. Dwiggins' brief vignette, "La Dernière Mobilisation" (*The Fabulist*, Autumn, 1915). Though the stories in the early series are always published in alphabetical order, by author, the juxtaposition of the two stories is quite striking. The story, which barely covers a printed page, depicts a gruesome scene that reads like a distant shot from a film. Emerging from a mist at the bottom of a hill is a "strange shadowy column that reaches slowly up the hill, moving in silence to the somber and muffled beating of a drum. As it draws nearer the shadow becomes two files of marching men bearing between them a long dim burden."[11] The men, clothed in a variety of uniforms, carry a series of interconnected planks which serve as a continuous litter of bodies covered by dirty, moldy blankets. Led by a soldier carrying a flagless staff, the column advances into the wood, eventually disappearing into the shadow: "There remain only the moonlight and the dusty hedgerow. From the left the road runs into Belgium; to the right it crosses into France. The dead were leaving their resting places in that lost land."[12] This motif of lines of dead will recur in a later story written by another author.

Though the stories here are all written in the first 15 months of the war, they pull no punches in regard to its hopelessness. Virgil Jordan goes even further, flashing forward in the malaise to 1916. In Jordan's "Vengeance is Mine" (*Everybody's Magazine*, April, 1915), another first person narrator tells the story of being stuck in the trenches, overlooking the Moselle, 15 miles from Metz. The narrator, who knows a little about the psychology of dreams by a "German psychologist," first speaks of the mindless tedium of the trenches: "our work had been each day to do so much digging, hauling, figuring, firing into the air, mechanically protecting ourselves from shells that we took as a matter of course, like wind and rain. We did not know when we had won a point against the unseen enemy. We did not feel their resistance as one feels a push."[13] In the boredom there was endless time for talk, particularly talk about the war: "Every evening we tried Germany over again, put her culture, commerce, social system on the rack, found her guilty and had her hanged, drawn, and quartered."[14]

It is now Christmas Eve, 1914, and, after an early night of shelling from the Germans, our narrator falls "into a long dreamy sleep." His dream takes him forward two years to Christmas Eve, 1916: "Two long, haggard years of the war had dragged by, to a wailing crescendo of misery, famine, disease, and madness. We had been hurled up and down an invisible line of death, bending and pressing it back and forth like a horde of ants at a thread." [15]The men no longer live like humans, but "like strange bees in an unknown place, sexless, unconscious in our activity, destroying instead of building . . . . All memory of another life was sunk deep into the subconscious. . . . Birth and death had lost their meaning."[16]

In this macabre atmosphere "[t]he carnival of chaos had spread like a wanton dementia."[17] Italy, Rumania, and Greece had entered the war. The countries of Europe had scrambled to claim German and Austrian territories. Germany was near defeat: "Russia debouched her million after million upon the east, and though they died dumbly like flies before the German walls of steel . . . they swept the Germans back over the Vistula and out of East Prussia . . . . There was not a German vessel left on the seven seas."[18]

Finally, on that Christmas Eve, the world was to make its final assault on Germany. The allied troops advanced across the Rhine, no longer met by steel resistance. They encountered bodies "not long dead." The Germans lay beneath a new fallen snow in tattered full-dress uniforms:

> fallen at a moment, at a word, hands here and there stiffened in a salute to the flag slow moving in the graying winter's dawn. Death we had seen, —but here in the streets and in the houses, in all corners and in all byways, the vivid faces of those who had sought death freely, each face telling with ghastly eloquence a tale that had never been told in the life of man of a race self-destroyed at a moment, at a word, for a vision which it alone had understood, leaving its epitaph in the words on the poison vials which a government machine efficient to the last had supplied—"Der Tag ist zu uns"—"The Day is Ours."[19]

In the stunning åftermath of their discovery, the troops come upon a new question to ponder: "Germany is yours, O Sons of Men! What now?"[20] The narrator then wakes from his dream to "the boisterous, bold boom of the batteries of Metz. They seemed to speak in glorious, wide-mouthed joy of Til Eulenspiegel and the young Siegfried. I thanked God for the Germans."[21] The prospect of Germany's total annihilation, even at the close of this terrible war, is unthinkable. The cost of total victory, even for the exhausted, would-be victor, is too much. Ironically, his dream victory, as in Comfort's story, is two years shy of the war's actual end. Though early in the war, Germany is already paying a horrible price, as seen in the next story, Mary Boyle O'Reilly's "In Berlin" (*Boston Daily Advertiser*, 22 December 1915).

Her story, the final war story from 1915, is yet another vignette. The story is so brief that I'll include it in its entirety:

> The train crawling out of Berlin was filled with women and children, hardly an able bodied man. In one compartment a gray-haired Landsturm soldier sat beside an elderly woman who seemed weak and ill. Above the click-clack of the car wheels passengers could hear her counting "One, two, three," evidently absorbed in her own thoughts. Sometimes she repeated the words at short intervals. Two girls tittered, thoughtlessly exchanging vapid remarks about such extraordinary behavior. An elderly man scowled reproval. Silence fell.
>
> "One, two, three," repeated the obviously unconscious woman. Again the girls giggled stupidly. The gray Landsturm leaned forward.
>
> "Fraulein," he said gravely, "you will perhaps cease laughing when I tell you that this poor lady is my wife. We have just lost our three sons in battle. Before leaving for the front myself I must take their mother to an insane asylum."
>
> It became terribly quiet in the carriage.[22]

This story depicts a desperate Germany, doomed to defeat and resigned to continued, senseless slaughter. With such scenes coming out in the first year of the war it is no wonder that the United States sought to stay out of the conflict.

*Best Short Stories* was silent regarding the war in 1916, but one disquieting story appears in 1917, Fanny Kemble Johnson's "The Strange-Looking Man" (*The Pagan*, December 1916). We are presented with a scene in a small mountain town from which "the men had gone forth to fight." The only men left in the village were the "very aged, and the bodily incapacitated." Of the men left in the village, we are provided with an eerie scene:

> One young man had only a part of a face, and had to wear a painted tin mask, like a holiday-maker. Another had two legs but no arms, and another had two arms, but no legs. One man could scarcely be looked at by his own mother, having had his eyes burned out of his head until he stared like Death. One had neither arms nor legs, and was mad of his misery besides, and lay all day in a cradle like a baby. . . . To go through that village after the war was something like going through a life-sized toy-village with all the mechanical figures wound up and clicking. Only instead of the figures being new and gay, and pretty, they were battered and grotesque and inhuman.[23]

The protagonist of this story is a three year-old boy, who possessed a "roving disposition." He wanders about the village, visiting the men, "the wrecks of the war which the Government of that country had made." The boy "tried on the tin mask, and played with the baker's mechanical leg . . . and it amused him excessively to rock the cradle of the man who had no limbs, and who was his father."[24] One morning, as his mother was busy with laundry, the child wanders out of the village along the bank of a mountain stream. There, near a deep pool, the child spies a "beautiful young man" swimming. The child watches as the man dresses after his swim:

> He had two arms, two legs, a whole face with eyes, nose, mouth, chin, and ears, complete. He could see, for he glanced about him as he dressed. He could speak, for he sang loudly. He could hear, for he had turned quickly at the whir of pigeon wings behind him. His skin was smooth all over, and nowhere on it were the dark scarlet maps which the child found so interesting on the arms, face, and breast of the burned man. He did not strangle every little while, or shiver madly, and scream at a sound.[25]

The child begins to whimper in terror and, when the man speaks to him, flees to the village screaming. The man follows him and, seeing him comforted by his mother, apologizes for frightening the boy. His mother replies: "It is because he finds the Herr Traveler so strange-looking. . . . He is quite small . . . and it is the first time he has even seen a whole man."[26] The irony in this story certainly emphasizes the dire situation in Europe. It seems so much more powerful when one considers that it is written two years before the end of the war.

The tone of these first five stories is impersonal, distanced. The main rhetorical motif is depiction. The writer does not take a position in so many words. Rather, the events of the story are depicted in such a strong fashion that the reader is drawn to an inevitable conclusion. The writers are troubled by the pathos and madness of the war, but there is little involvement. The situations exist, but without apparent reason. The stories describe a distant world gone awry. That world is European, not American, and remains an ocean away. Commentary on the war is unnecessary. The United States was not involved. The depictions, the word pictures, of the war in Europe speak for themselves. By 1918, however, with the US firmly involved in the war, the tone of the stories changes. The struggle in Europe is heightened to one of spiritual significance. The carnage takes place for unworldly reasons. Spirits and ironies appear right and left. Indeed, O'Brien noted in 1918 that he had read "several hundred war stories" and found that "fully sixty per cent . . . dealt with some supernatural aspect of the war."[27] Eventually, some of the stories come to portray an American cause infused with American values, stubbornness, common sense, and legends.

## Spirits, Supercargo, and Voices

With the United States fully immersed (the United States declared war in April 1917), no less than seven of the stories from 1918 address the war. The tone begins to become one of patriotism, though in somewhat fantastical form at

times. The war itself starts to become elevated to an action of spiritual significance; each story is a morality tale.

Mary Mitchell Freedley's "Blind Vision" (*The Century Magazine*, 1 January 1918) gives a glimpse of the war outside the trenches, in the air. And it portrays the code of honor that was still adhered to by airmen in the Great War. The
narrator tells of a November meeting with Marston, who with his friend Esme
had visited the narrator the previous summer, both "vitally alive." On this day,
however, Marston appears as a different man," a stone-sculptured image of the
gay, glad boy I had known."[28] Marston is distraught. He has searched for weeks
to find "some one—you, any one who knew us" to whom he could relate a story.[29]

Another friend, Brender, had crashed near the British lines and was near
death. He had asked to see Esme. Esme flew off in a Nieuport (not a fighter)
across the German lines to see his friend. Along the way he is engaged by a
German fighter plane. Rather than attempt to outrun the German, Esme engaged
in a dogfight. Ultimately, he tried to ram the other plane and they fall to the
earth together. Their escadrille is moved by Esme's gallant effort and, in tribute,
dropped a memorial wreath, bearing his name, behind the German lines. The
Germans replied with a message of their own. One of their planes flew over the
French lines and dropped a stone: "Painted on it in German was, 'Your dead
sends thanks!'" The narrator comments, "That's just like them, brutal, and the
last word on their side."[30]

A month later a plane appeared from across the lines and begins to do a
series of aerobatic stunts, ones characteristic of Esme. The French allowed the
plane to land and, miraculously, it was Esme, who had survived the crash.

He had been taken prisoner by the Germans, tortured, and eventually forced
to fly over the French lines with a photographer. At one point in the flight Esme
noticed that the photographer's harness was loosened. He pulled the plane into a
series of somersaults and spins and dropped the photographer to his death. Marston was appalled when he heard the tale. Esme had broken the aviator's code of
honor:

> Some times one forgets to guard one's expression. I suppose mine showed the
> horror I couldn't help feeling. He put his hand out to touch me, but I jumped up
> and moved away. . . .
> "Marston," he said, "What's the matter? Aren't you glad? There wasn't any
> other way but to give in to them. . . . What was his life among so many? It's
> war, Marston; war."[31]

Marston could not respond adequately. "I didn't stop to think of his over
wrought condition, mentally and physically. He simply wasn't responsible."[32]
Marston knew that Esme's explanation would not suffice for the other men: "We
have a code all our own; no rules, no mention ever made of its interpretation—
just an aviator's honor." Marston rejected Esme, pointing out his violation: "it
wasn't the way we fought to drop a man thousands of feet who was only doing

his duty. It was murder. . . . He wasn't my friend, he was a murderer."[33] Marston, after ten minutes of thought, reconsidered his response and searched for his friend, but he had gone, presumably behind enemy lines, and left a note:

> In other branches of the service what I did would have gone, been all right, been smart. . . . because we've chosen to have a different, a higher standard, because we fight cleanly, what I did was dirty. Well, I understand. . . . I go to render unto Caesar. A life for a life. To give them at least my death, since I can no longer offer even that proudly to France.[34]

The narrator closes the story with the image of Marston: "I only remember the broken stem of his glass, the stain that was spreading slowly over the white cloth, and the dripping, dripping red of his hands."[35] The story highlights the well-chronicled chivalry of the air war in Europe. While troops on the ground slaughtered each other with modern weapons, the air warriors, flying the most modern weapon of all, cling to a code of honor from the past. Honor code or none, war is still Hell. Though it can be conducted as a game,the consequences are quite real, as the next story demonstrates as well.

G. Humphrey's "The Father's Hand" (*The Bookman*, June, 1918) is yet another story told second hand. It explores a senseless aspect of the war, through a horrible irony. The irony itself is presented through a discussion of "dead" languages and literature that signals an end of an era, but not its total dismissal. In this case the narrator is dining with an Oxford Dean and the conversation touches on the prospect for teaching Latin poetry after the war is over. The Dean responds with an anecdote about a Latin verse, "*Bis patriae manus cecidere*," which refers to the death of Icarus' father. The Dean knew of a stone carver from Alsace-Loraine with whom he would often chat in Latin phrases of the type carved on monuments. The stone carver had lived in Alsace-Loraine during French governance and was a bitter opponent of Germany. Nothing specific was known of his past, save that he had once been married and that his wife had died in childbirth.

The Dean's village was a regular recipient of air raids and the old stone carver, an observant man, had determined a regular flight pattern. He came up with a plan to shoot down one of the "German pigs," as he calls them. The plan works and English gunners successfully shoot down a German plane. "Fuit Ilium. [Troy is fallen] The German is destroyed,"[36] the stone cutter cries in triumph.

The old stone cutter becomes something of a local hero because of his successful plan. The villagers decide to bury the body of the aviator in the local cemetery. What should the inscription be? In spite of the carver's preference for a Latin inscription, the village decides to inscribe merely "here lies a fallen German"[37] on the stone. Continuing the celebration, remnants from the dead aviator's effects are displayed in the village museum. There was no identification or address for the flier, but there was a picture of a young woman, inscribed "meine mutter." The Dean dropped by the stone cutter's shop to ask what he thought of the exhibit. The old man was found lying on the ground, chisel on the ground next to his empty hand, the tombstone uninscribed. The old man falls into a precipitous decline. He can no longer work. Eventually, the monument is placed in the graveyard unmarked.

Sometime later the Dean goes to view the grave and there finds the old carver dead near the stone of the German aviator on which he had carved a partial inscription: "Bis patriae m . . . Twice the hands of the father failed. The dead man was his son."[38] Again, emphasis is on European madness, a sentiment still shared by an America reluctantly arming for war. Nonetheless, like the killing of the German aviator, the war has become a necessary action.

Frances Gilchrist Wood's "The White Battalion" (*The Bookman*, 17 May 1918) presents yet another foray into the supernatural. The scene is a post-battle debriefing between officers of the French army and American officers of the French Foreign Legion. Under discussion is a forty-second delay in an attack led by French officers in charge of female soldiers. The women, widows of French soldiers, had been inspired by Russian women to form their own unit. Though the French military had repeatedly refused their efforts to fight, the women persisted and the group was finally accepted into the army and trained as soldiers. Each woman was issued a packet of cyanide of potassium with her equipment to hasten the inevitable death that awaited them in the trenches. The women requested that they be allowed to retake the position for which their husbands had died defending earlier in the war, in 1914. As the women charged across No Man's Land toward the German trenches they were stopped, motionless, by an appalling sight:

> Thrust shield-wise above the heads of the Huns, crowning the ditch as if with protective spikes, frightened and sobbing, cowering before us were hundreds of little children! . . .
> The Huns had thrust their guns between the children, and were holding their fire—the devilish cat and mouse game![39]

One of the women soldiers, who were called the "Avengers," then made the sign of the cross, their "voiceless" battle cry: "She lifted her right hand in the sweep of victory—on her wrist was bound the packet of death they carry in case of capture by the Kultur beasts—and fell, for the Huns opened fire the instant they saw her gesture."[40] The gesture communicated to the women that they must continue the charge and the cyanide "would erase the memory forever."[41] The men, meanwhile, looked on at the action with "the look of the face of Christ on the cross!"[42] Suddenly, however, a mist, "a battalion of marching shadows in a blur of the old red and blue [early French uniform colors in the Great War]" charged in front of the Avengers and decimated the German troops, without harming the children. The Avengers, meanwhile, gathered the captive children up in their arms. Several of the male officers recognized among the pale ghosts, the faces of their old comrades. An American Legionnaire confirmed that it was "like the fog blowing in off Frisco bay . . . ."[43]

The Germans had taunted the French by saying their army had been bled white. A French officer summarized their response:

> And France bled white . . . . [sic] we know, "the words halted, the country for which we went to war is maimed—scarred—she can never again be the same France, but—"his face gleamed through the dim light," our battle cry has changed! We no longer fight *'Pour la Patrie!* But 'Pour le Droit!'—the right that is greater than country." . . . the fouling Beast is going in the end—we know! He cannot stand against the unconquerable dead. And when we march at the head of the column—"he lifted his hand in salute, "Pour le Droit!"[44]

Reinvigorated, the officers marched off to headquarters. The tone is again noble, and certainly not one of futility. Gone is the depiction of the war as European madness. The war now has taken on spiritual significance. The portrayal of the Germans in these stories also takes on a new twist. Gone are the sympathetic portrayals. Germany has now become "brutal," and "a fouling beast."

Katharine Prescott Moseley's "The Story Vinton Heard at Mallorie" (*Scribners*, September, 1918), also features the supernatural, this time in opposition to "hideous work." A young war correspondent has returned to his friends in New England. In response to queries about the nature of things in Europe he becomes philosophic, indeed theological: 'Everything over there—I mean all sorts of what you'd call merely material objects—is being charged with some kind of spiritual essence that is going to be indefinitely active to future contact."[45] His friends, solid, pragmatic Yankees, cannot relate to his topic. Ultimately, he relates a story that was told to him.

Vinton had become acquainted with the family of the Marquis of Mallorie, a high-church family, scarcely protestant, who maintained a chapel on their estate. The son of the family had been killed in the war and, eventually, his body was interred in the chapel. On the anniversary of the brother's death, a twelve hour vigil was kept at the chapel and at 3:00 AM the following incident occurred. A zeppelin appeared hovering over the chapel, so near that one "could see the crew and their preparation for the hideous work afoot."[46] As the teller of the story, the slain soldier's sister, watches in horror, an "aeroplane" appears and, reaching the zeppelin, begins circling around it. "It seemed as if the aeroplane was winding the monster in some intangible net, in which it turned and twisted and writhed, trying to get away into the free air; and then, again without a single shot, it fell to the earth."[47]

The "aeronaut" responsible for this grand deed lands on the grounds nearby. In the early morning light his hair was golden and he appeared to be clad in black armor. The young pilot, Lt. Templar, stays with the Mallories for a while, as his aeroplane is in need of repairs. Later that week a General dines with the Mallories and, after a private conversation with Lt. Templar, announces: "The young saviour of Mallorie Abbey may be the saviour of Europe."[48] Shortly afterward, the daughter engages Templar in conversation. Why, she asks, was he able to bring the great Zeppelin down without a single shot? He replies:

Because in me is all the strength of that bright ardor which has led young warriors to die in battle for the right since earth began. And now my strength is
most mightily a renewal with the strength of the lads who were the first to die
for England. Was not your brother one of these? Such souls are the stuff of
which are made the angels and archangels and all the heavenly host.[49]

As she looks at him it seems as if his evening clothes have been transformed
into the black armor he was wearing when she first saw him. She asks him who
he is and "he, like Lohengrin, was gone." From that day forward there "has been
no more sorrowing at Mallorie Abbey." Vinton closes his tale, remarking, "They
have never known which of them it was, Michael—or Gabriel—or Raphael!"[50]

When asked by his hosts if he believes the story, Vinton responds: "When I
remember that all the trouble on this earth comes in the train of that infernal
thing we call the ego it seems to me that the heavenly things must indeed arise
from its complete surrender. Yes—, yes I think that I like it very much."[51] Such
an epic struggle has to be the stuff of knights and angels. Again, the tone is noble, spiritual, and uplifting, and certainly not futile.

The war also becomes an American war in the stories of 1918. Again, the
common theme is spiritual, though in a particularly American fashion. Harrison
Rhodes' "Extra Men" (*Harpers*, July, 1918) features the events occurring on
Burridge Road, near Princeton, New Jersey: "But with the coming of the Great
War strange things are stirring in the world, and in the farthest corners of the
land the earth is shaken by the tramp of new armies. . . . and things one does not
believe can happen may be happening, even in New Jersey."[52] Our narrator,
stranded in the locale because his car has broken down, tells of "old Mrs. Buchan," in whose house George Washington had stayed on his way to join his
armies in New York. Mrs. Buchan's grandson, George, has enlisted in the avia-
tion service. Two days before his departure for France he visits his grandmother
to say goodbye.

After young George's departure, around dusk, a man knocks at Mrs. Buchan's door: "He was in riding-breeches and gaiters and a rather old-fashioned
riding-coat. And in the band of his hat he had stuck a small American flag which
looked oddly enough almost like a cockade."[53] The visitor, after bowing and
removing his hat, speaks to Mrs. Buchan in the "softer accents of Virginia and
the states farther south" and asks for directions. Mrs. Buchan points the way to
Princeton and the visitor replies: "Princeton, of course. That's where we fought
the British and beat them. It seems strange, does it not, that we must now fight
with them."[54]

The visitor indicates that he must be in New York by morning so that he
may sail to France. Mrs. Buchan responds, pointing out that her grandson,
George Buchan, is also on his way to serve in France. The visitor remarks:

"George Buchan? There was a George Buchan fought at Princeton I remember."

"There was. And another George Buchan in the War of 1812. And a John in the Mexican War. And William in eighteen sixty three. There was no one in the Spanish War—my son was dead and my grandson too young. But now he is ready."

"Every American is ready," her visitor answered. "I am ready. . . .

Every one who has ever fought for America is going. There is a company of them behind me. Listen."[55]

From up the road come men on horseback, dressed in uniforms of various hues. Mrs. Buchan allows the horses to graze in her meadow and the visitor whom Mrs. Buchan now addresses as "General" partakes of Sherry and sponge-cake.

Before the General departs Mrs. Buchan tells him that he will know her boy and that young George will know him as well. The General replies:

I want them all to know that I am there," he had replied. "They will know. They will remember their country's history even as we now remember. And when the shells scream in the French sky they will not forget the many times America has fought for liberty. They will not forget those early soldiers. And they will not forget Grant and Lee and Lincoln. The American Eagle, madam, has a very shrill note. I think it can be heard above the whistle of German shrapnel."[56]

The General and his troops depart and the next morning a local farmer is surprised to find Mrs. Buchan's wheat field trampled down. Not many people believe Mrs. Buchan's story, our narrator tells us, "But old Mrs. Buchan believes that with each American troop-ship there will sail supercargo, extra men. And she believes that with those extra men, we cannot lose the fight."[57] Now, American civic spirituality is fully fused into the war literature.

In 1918 William Dudley Pelley's "The Toast to Forty-Five" (*The Pictorial Review*, May, 1918) returns again to the Grand Army of the Republic. This time, however, the story connects the G. A. R. with troops departing for World War I in a grand, patriotic, and Christian fable. The Forty-Five was a ritual of the proud G. A. R. Company of Paris, Vermont, which served with distinction during the Civil War In August, 1866, veterans from the company met to commemorate their triumph. Captain Jack Fuller had risen and given a toast to his comrades, "the forty-five brave lads who marched away with us but who were not destined by a higher providence to march back."[58] Each year, he noted, their annual gathering would be smaller. He held up an unopened bottle of the wine being consumed at that gathering. He proposed that the bottle remain unopened until the last survivor would drink a toast to all who had gone before them. Ironically, Captain Jack, himself, was dead by the next reunion.

The story moves forward to 1912. Only four of the original company remain alive and Jack Fuller, grandson of the original Captain Jack, is in trouble. In the culmination of a misspent youth, he has come home drunk and accidentally knocked the cradle holding his nine-months-old baby to the floor. The blow has killed the child. In desperation he vows to his young, heart-stricken wife, that he'll never touch a drop of liquor again. He keeps his vow, but as the war in Europe comes closer, he yearns to serve as his father and grandfather had before him. His wife, Betty, still suffers from the loss of their child and has begged Jack not to enlist in the National Guard. Jack agrees, but eventually organizes a local company of men, the Paris Home Guard, whom he serves as Captain. The subject of military service is again raised between Jack and Betty, and this time she falls into a bout of hysteria that requires medical attention. The Doctor warns Jack that, should he enlist, the shock might kill his wife.

The United States entered the war in April, 1917, and by the following August the G. A. R. celebration was at hand. Only one veteran of the G. A. R., Joe Fodder remained. The town wanted the Paris Home Guard to announce their enlistment at the annual G. A. R. dinner. Young Jack agrees. Reluctantly, his wife attends the banquet.

Sam Hod, editor of the local newspaper, presided over the dinner. He recounted the glorious history of the Paris company and transitioned to a summary of President Wilson's reasons for America's entry into the current conflict. He then summarized Captain Jack's toast from fifty-two years before and passed on a request from the two remaining survivors of the G. A. R. Company:

> It has been suggested that nothing could have more approval from Dashing Captain Jack himself—or from all of those one hundred and six brave men who have crossed from the battlefields of earthly life into blessed reward for their altruism—than that this toast should be given after all—if not by the two survivors, than by the leader of the local heroes who have volunteered to go "Over There" and by their sacrifice made the earth a finer, better place in which to dwell."[59]

The seal of the famous wine bottle was then broken and a glass of the precious wine poured for Joe Fodder and young Captain Jack Fuller. Old Joe, toothless, trembling, and spilling the wine on the table cloth "like a clot of blood," gives an awkward toast to Captain Jack Fuller and his posterity."[60] Joe could say no more, and young Captain Jack, the tragically childless grandson of his illustrious forebear, rose to his feet.

Young Captain Jack had not touched a drop of liquor in the six years since the unfortunate event that killed his only child. Two hundred people watched to see what he would do:

> Deliberately into his dirty coffee-cup he poured the blood-red liquid. As his grandfather would have done, with the same exaggerated flourish the boy took from his pocket a snow-white handkerchief. With that napkin he wiped flawlessly the delicate receptacle which had held the liquor. Then he leaned over. From a glass pitcher he poured into that cleansed wine-glass its fill of pure cold sparkling water. In an instant he held it aloft. "Fellows!" he cried. "A toast! A toast not with wine—for wine with its blood-color belongs to the times which are going—which we hope are passing forever—I'm drinking a toast with crys-

tal water—emblematic of the clean white civilization which is coming—for which we're going 'Over There' to fight and die."[61]

He then went on to deliver an oration that invoked the glory of the forty-five and the other brave men of '62, "who have gone to take finer and better orders under a Greater General, the Commander of Commanders, the Prince of—Peace!"[62] He toasted the mothers, the wives, and "the girls we are leaving behind!"[63] He toasted the nobility of those women, the same nobility of the one who bore the cross to Golgotha. He concluded: "These are the things to which we drink—the men of yesterday—and the memory of their heroism which has been—and the women of to-day and whose heroism is to be. With the great incentive of these two in our hearts, boys—let us drink and go away to fight like men—to honor the first—and to sanctify the second."[64]

The speech, declared an old lady present, was "almost word for word—the night John Farrington's company bade us women-folks goodbye."[65] Later, Betty, also overwhelmed by the spirit that infused the event, gives Jack her blessing: "'And you can count on me, Jack,' she said, 'I'll—do—my—duty—too. Even—if. You should never come back; remember I said—I was sorry for the way I've acted; I'll—do—my—duty—too.'" And, the narrator tells us, "she sent him away—with a smile!"[66]

Thus, Pelley's story fuses the fate of the doughboys with their blue-clad ancestors. He likens their sacrifice of war to the sacrifice of Christ. And finally, he makes the toast to the forty-five an act of communion and forgiveness for Jack and Betty Fuller. The melodramatic story features titles and lines from two popular songs in the war years, "Over There" and "Send Me Away with a Smile."

Ironies continue to probe the perverse premises of war. Fleta Campbell Springer's "Solitaire" (*Harpers*, January 1918) touches on the war, but more directly on heroism. This is another story related by another. Yet it strongly bears the mark of its female writer—a woman trying to understand men and their innate attraction to war. The narrator tells of a man he met in 1912, a man from Iowa, named Corey. He met Corey in a café in Paris. Corey was dressed in a Balkan uniform, yet stood out from the crowd as distinctly American. The remarkable thing about Corey, the thing that gathered his attention, was the six ribbons displayed on the breast of his uniform blouse: the Legion of Honor, the Japanese Order of the Rising Sun, and decorations from Russia and England. Corey hailed from Dubuque and was in Paris securing medical supplies for the Serbian army for whom he served as a doctor. The remarkable features of the young man were forgotten by the narrator until some years later, during the late stages of the Great War when he was traveling in the United States, west from Chicago. There he met a man named Ewing, who, as chance would have it, was the executor of Corey's estate. Dr. Corey had been killed in the war some three months earlier. From Ewing he learned the story of Corey's life. He had picked up his various decorations during the course of satisfying his medical curiosity. He had traveled to China to study herbal medicine and happened upon the Boxer

Rebellion. He joined the conflict, distinguishing himself through both medical and military efforts. There he was awarded the Legion of Honor and the Order of the Rising Sun. Later, after serving in the Balkan War, he came home to marry and settle down. When the Great War began he confounded everyone by staying home. Later, however, after supposedly going east for a medical conference in Philadelphia, he disappeared for a period of two months. When he came home he bore the Croix de Guerre. It turns out that Corey had a compulsion to seek action and do heroic deeds, an aspect of his personality he is unaware of until his wife confronts him with it after his two month absence. Corey returns to the war once more and, this time, deliberately places himself in the path of an exploding shell to save the lives of others. For this act he was to receive the Medaille Militaire. The catch was that the award is only given to living soldiers. Corey, clinging to life in a field hospital, refuses an injection that will help him live until a time when a general was scheduled to present the award. In his dying hours Corey asks that a message be sent to Ewing: "'Tell him,' he said, 'that it breaks a man's luck to know what he wants.'"[67] Ewing was further asked not to tell Corey's wife of the final honor. Both Ewing and the narrator are puzzled at Corey's refusal to take the medication and to inform his wife. Our narrator, however, finally hazards a guess: "Perhaps he had wished to spare her the pang of an added disgrace."[68] This story is something of a commentary on the war, neither futile nor hopeful. Rather, it seems to be a resigned commentary on the nature of men.

Yet another commentary is Julian Street's "Bird of Serbia," (*Collier's Weekly*) a piece reflecting on the passing of Gavrilo Prinzipe, whose assassination of Archduke Ferdinand is often counted as the cause of the Great War. Again, the impetus for the story is a remark from one man to another on a Pullman car. The conversation moves to the consideration of whether or not the young Serb's act had indeed been the cause of the war. One of the men gathered there carefully pointed out that the assassination took place in Austria-Hungary and was committed by an Austro-Hungarian subject. How, then, asked another man, could Austria-Hungary make the assassination the reason to start a war? His interlocutor, who had worked in southeastern Europe before the war, replies:

> "It was one of the poorest excuses imaginable," he returned. "Autocracies can do those things; that's why they must be stamped out. As you said, historians will trace back to the assassination—microscopic, unclean forces of which historians will never hear, yet which seem peculiarly suitable in connection with Austria's crime. But I had better not get to talking about all that."[69]

What follows, of course, is a story about what he learned during his time in southeast Europe. He spent much time in Serbia, learned the language, and stayed regularly in an Inn owned by a Serbian family in Bosnia, in a city populated by Serbs, "Mohammedans," and Austrians. Serbia and Bosnia were a part of the Serbian empire, but had been conquered by the Turks at Kosovo (which means field of the *Kos*—a type of black starling) in 1389 and, later, by Austria.

The father of the Serbian family with which he stayed was a pragmatist, who worked with the existing reign. His young son, Gavrilo, who had become the storyteller's friend, was the holder of radical, anti-Austrian attitudes.

When he became older, Gavrilo became betrothed to a beautiful neighbor girl, Mara. Their relationship, however, is somewhat tempestuous, particularly in regard to Gavrilo's Serbian nationalism.

Shortly before the celebration of Kosovo Day, June 28, our narrator visits Mara, who is sewing in her garden. In a bird cage hanging nearby is a *kos*, the little bird for whom the battlefield was named. Our narrator is surprised at the sight because the *kos* is not a domesticatable bird. He and Mara have an exchange which apparently mirrors one between Mara and Gavrilo at an earlier time. Gavrilo had begged her to release the bird, which had been a gift from an elder relative of Mara's, but Mara steadfastly refused. As the narrator and Mara are talking, Gavrilo bursts into the garden and announces that the Archduke has canceled the Kosovo Day celebrations because of army maneuvers nearby which must be viewed by him. The narrator is surprised by the development, noting that the Archduke is widely seen as pro-Serb and is married to a Slav. Gavrilo replies angrily:

> He is the spawn of an autocrat who is in turn the spawn of generations of autocrats. Scratch them and they are all the same. They play the evil game of empire—the dirty game of holding together, against their will, the people of seven races in Austria-Hungary; grinding them down, humiliating them, keeping them afraid. No man, no group of men, should have such power! It is medieval, grotesque, wicked![70]

After his tirade, Mara reminds him that he has promised that as long as she loves him, he will not involve himself in violent activities. Then, he asks her to release the *kos* as a sign of her love. She refuses and the couple engages in yet another row.

Eventually, the bird dies from parasites and the two lovers quarrel as to who is responsible for the bird's death. When the young woman learns from a trusted authority that the *kos'* death was indeed caused by its captivity, she begs the narrator to find Gavrilo and tell him that she does truly love him. It is too late. Our narrator witnesses Gavrilo's assassination of the Archduke.

The end of the story brings a stunned silence in the rail car. The narrator resumes his tale with a homily:

> historians will doubtless trace the beginnings of the war to Gavrilo's shot. Certainly Austria used the shot as her excuse, alleging that the plot to kill the Archduke had been hatched in Serbia—which was absolutely untrue, for Serbia was afraid of nothing as much as of giving offense to Austria, knowing well that Austria was only seeking a pretense to pounce upon her, precisely as she had earlier pounced upon Bosnia and Herzegovina, annexing them.
>
> . . . . I am glad to know that [Gavrilo] is free at last. Like Mara's starling, he was not one to live long in a cage. And it is perhaps because I was so fond of

him, and also because Austria's excuse was so transparently despicable, that I shall always go behind the shooting in thinking of the beginning of the war.[71]

He goes on to speak of Marta's anger with Gavrilo, brought on by the death of the bird. One of his companions interjects—you mean the cause of the war was due to the "death of that caged bird?" The storyteller replies: "rather . . . to a still smaller and more repulsive beginning—to the vermin which destroyed the bird. It seems to me I see them always crawling through the explanations, apologies, excuses, war messages, and peace overtures of the Teutonic autocrats."[72] The commentary, speaking to the entangled political and military alliances of pre-war Europe, strikes something of a blow against the European madness.

Understandably, stories about the war have all but disappeared in the 1919 volume (though the issue includes stories published as late as November, 1918). Maxwell Strother Burt's "The Blood Red One" (*Scribner's*, November , 1918) however, provides a powerful retrospective on the war and continues the supernatural theme. In this tale, another second hand account, "old Mr. Vandusen" has gone to his club to interact with a group of friends in the library. As he sits in his comfortable chair in the dimly lit room he overhears a discussion between several men about the state of the world as a result of modern technology. Technology, they observe, has interrupted the natural order involving evil and punishment. One man, Tomlinson, pontificates:

No, there is something wrong, some break in the rhythm of the universe, or those full-bodied, cold-blooded hangmen, who for forty years have been sitting back planning the future of men and women as they planned the cards of their sniggering skat games, would awake to a sun dripping blood." He paused for a moment. "And as for that psychiatric cripple, their mouthpiece," he concluded somberly, "that maimed man who broods over battle-fields, he would find a creeping horror in his brain like death made visible."[73]

Suddenly, from the darkness of the dimly lit room, a voice inquires: "And you think he will not?" . . . ." The voice, "extraordinary," and "like a bell" brings silence to the room and the voice relates several vignettes.

The first takes place in a beech forest in a sunny early November where six motor cars proceed to a hunting lodge. The cars bear "the Maimed Man" and his entourage. We first meet the Maimed Man in the lodge, where he is attended by a servant who has only one arm. Upon being questioned by his master, he replies that he lost the arm at Liege. The Maimed Man asks plaintively, "Can I not escape such things even here?"[74]

The "voice" then proceeds to tell two more stories about the Maimed Man. The first he calls "the story of the leaves that marched." In this scene the Maimed Man walks deep into the woods, ahead of his attendants. Only a lone huntsman accompanies the Maimed Man as he sits pensively in woods around sunset: "'Here they come!' said the Maimed Man suddenly. 'I see gray moving. There—below there, amongst the trees!' . . . . Moving across the calm forest, not blown, but moving slowly, were "Gray leaves, creeping forward with a curious dogged languor. And when they come to the brook they paused on its farther edge and stopped, and the ones behind came pushing up to them. And looking down upon them, they might have been the backs of wounded men in gray, dragging themselves on their knees to water. . . ."[75] Then, from across a clearing, a figure of an "upstanding man" appears. He looks toward the Maimed Man and signals a group behind him. This group marches with precision across the clearing:

> As they trampled upon the stricken leaves by the brookside the fixed stare in the Maimed Man's eyes faded, and he watched them with vivid attention. Shortly they came to where he had got to his feet. A huge elderly man with a red face led them.
> "But your majesty," he objected, "it is not fitting. You should not leave us in this way. Even here is it altogether safe?"[76]

The voice continues and offers a third anecdote, called "the mist that came up suddenly."

The Maimed Man has finished his dinner and, leaving the table, walks to a balcony to savor a cigar. As he gazed out to enjoy the moonlight he was enveloped by a "swirling vapor that in an instant lost him completely from the door he had just left; a maelstrom of fog, that choked him, half blinded him, twisted about him like wet, coiling ropes, and in a dreadful moment he saw that through the fog were thrust out toward him arms of a famine thinness, the extended fingers of which groped at his throat, were obliterated by the fog, groped once more with a searching intentness."[77]

After the Maimed Man struggles a bit, the mist withdraws, but the Maimed Man cannot take his eyes of the mist "for it seemed to him that the open place was filled with the despairing arms of women and of children, and that through the shifting whiteness gleamed the whiteness of their serried faces."[78] The Maimed Man could not go back into the room. He needed to compose himself.

"'For you see," said the voice, and in the darkness its accent took on a glow, rhythmical somberness, like the swish of a sword in a shuttered room," this was far worse than the leaves. For after all, the dead are only the dead, but to the living there is no end."[79] Without a further word, the voice stops. None of the men in the room ever sees him, nor does anyone see him leave the room. It is interesting that this story was told in an allegorical style and with the Kaiser's identity (he was born with a withered arm) obscured. Its purpose seems to be more of an eerie morality tale than a denunciation of a particular person.

The war returns in the 1923 volume, again with a supernatural theme, in Dana Burnett's "Beyond the Cross," (*The Pictorial Review*, February, 1923). The story's unnamed narrator, a former reporter, now a playwright, is sailing for France on an ocean liner. He swears to himself that he sees a man on board whose face is the same of a former colleague, Philip Trainor, who was killed in France during the war. The other man approaches the narrator the next day.

They had both worked on the Evening Herald, though at different times. The man, who introduces himself as Jim White, brings up his resemblance to Trainor: "Everyone in the shop thought I looked like Trainor."[80] When asked if he had served in the war White responds that he doesn't know. He then proceeds to confide in the narrator that he has no recollection of his past. Jim White was a name he made up when he applied for the job at the Evening Herald. After he started work he found out that he resembled the man named Trainor. White begins to realize that he and Trainor have a lot in common and begins to see Trainor in his dreams. The dream is always the same. He goes to meet Trainor and always finds him just out of reach "in the fog—beyond the cross."[81]

White is now sailing for France for reasons for which he is not quite sure. But he knows he will visit Trainor's grave. White is entrapped in a mystery, he feels: "It's as if I were about to solve the riddle of the universe."[82]

The two travel to Paris together and then, after being apart for two weeks, White reappears at our narrator's lodgings. He has visited Trainor's grave, near Reims. Having seen the destroyed cathedral at Reims, he remarks that he "couldn't help thinking what a monument it was to the futility of all religions. It'll be much better when we substitute knowledge for religion." At Trainor's grave White could not see how the earth could contain a "thing" so fine and variable as the human spirit." White senses that Trainor "was gone out of his flesh to some other plane."[83] That night White dreams of Trainor and this time meets him through the fog.

The next day, White meets another man at the cemetery, the father of one of the other aviators who had died with Trainor. The man tells him that his son and Trainor had been good friends when they trained near Betancourt. That evening White tells the narrator that he will travel to Betancourt the next day. He also reveals to the narrator that he thinks Trainor's spirit has entered his body.

Weeks pass as our narrator continues his stay in Paris, musing from time to time on the mystery of Trainor and White. Finally, while dining alone at his café he is approached by White, who has returned from Balincourt. In Balincourt he learns of Mlle. Bosquanet, daughter of a wealthy manufacturer, who remained in the village, a reclusive single mother: "It was rumored that she had lost her husband in the war."[84]

White is led to visit Mlle. Bosquanet. He meets her three-year old son in the garden and, upon learning that White is an American, the boy takes White to his mother. White feels a "pain" in his heart upon meeting Mlle. Bosquanet. Mlle. Bosquanet reacts to him with no emotion and sends him away. White, however, is so disturbed by this encounter that he returns to Mlle. Bosquanet's home the next day. This time they have a brief conversation. He tells her that he lost something in the war. She reveals that she lost both parents. She concludes their conversation by inviting him back to tea the next day.

This time Mlle. Bosquanet is dressed gaily, as she had before the war, and they engage in general, but happy, conversation. A thunderstorm comes and they go inside the house. Mlle. Bosquanet's mood darkens with the storm. Her son, frightened by the storm, comes to her for comfort and is then led away by her nurse. White asks if the boy's father had been killed in the war. She looks at White for a while and asks who he is. White replies that he is a man who has lost his memory. She becomes quite emotional: "You are he!" . . . . "Philip, Philip."[85]

White tells Mlle. Bosquanet that he is not Trainor, but that he has been searching for her. She asks if he has a message for her. He doesn't know. They then exchange life stories in hopes that a message will be revealed. She loved Trainor, but he was sent away before they could marry. She later bore his child. It turns out, however, that Trainor had never told her that he loved her. Mlle. Bosquanet reveals that this one question above all her travails continues to plague her. White replies in words that "lay in my consciousness as clear as sunlight. . . . He hears—and waits . . . . He will be at your side when you fall asleep at last. . . . You will go with him through the fog on the other side of the cross."[86] White leaves her as she gently weeps. The next day he returns to Paris and tells his story to our narrator.

Hearing it all, the narrator asks: "How does it answer your problem?" White stares at him with a bewildered look and glances frantically around the café. "What am I doing here? My God it's stifling. This room is like a coffin."[87] He quickly leaves the room and, though our narrator rushes to follow him, disappears. When the narrator asks M. Druot, who was sitting in the café, and had seen them together many times, if he saw which way White had gone, Druot replies, "No one has gone out."[88] Trainor's restless spirit, like many in the Great War, is eventually put to rest, but not without great struggle.

A more traditional spiritual resolution is seen in Solon K. Stewart's "The Contract of Corporal Twing" (Harper's, February, 1923), also in 1923. Stewart's story takes the war to another region, sixty miles from Baghdad. Corporal Elijah Twing and two colleagues are all that remain of a detachment ambushed in a pass, high above the desert. They have been holding out against snipers until they can be rescued after dark. Twing, a profane, little cockney, is contemptuous of British, Turks, Christians, and Moslems whom he holds responsible for the war. One man has already been killed by a sniper and the second is severely wounded. Twing signals for help and tries to withstand the heat and the enemy. In desperation he sends out yet another plea for help, flashing Morse Code with a hand mirror:

> God this is corporal Twing expert signaler passed out Canterbury AAA I here on bloody rock my mate private Carson wounded AAA Rest of us gone West Some of them will get to you AAA God I said I didn't believe in you I don't now AAA get my mate out of this bleeding mess and I believe in you AAA It's a bargain AAA God it ain't for myself I say this AAA It is laid down that NCO at all times see to comfort and safety of men in their charge AAA So I got to get him to British lines AAA It's a damn hard job AAA God give me the guts to carry on what I'm a doing of and carry on     Corporal Twing signaler[89]

The British troops, who all read the message as it is slowly flashed before them, quickly mobilize to save their comrades. The Turks, who can see but not understand the message, conclude that the message is a call to battle and meet the British troops on the pass. After the battle, Twing is found, nearly trampled to death, shielding the body of his wounded colleague. Twing asks an officer to help him get over to the body of his dead comrade:

> "I'd like the sergeant to 'elp me up there—to that perishing ledge. My dead mate's up there—Perkins. . . ."
> "Well?"
> "Well, sir, I been a bit of a rotter—but I bloody well 'ave to keep a contrack, bein' a N.C. O., 'aven't I?
> "Could you, sir?" and his drawn, haggard cheeks were suffused, as a shame-faced expression flitted across his face, to leave his jaw set doggedly. "I'd like to stay there arf a mo by myself, sir, afore they tykes me to the bleedin' 'orspital.
> "I want to kneel by my mate to say me—prayers."[90]

Twigg's "foxhole" conversion, the staple of so many war stories, comes across less in a spiritual sense and more in the sense of honoring a promise. It is a fitting transition to stories of a more cynical tone. The more cynical stories to come are about the Great War, but writers are still recalling the Civil War in fond, romantic terms.

F. J. Stimson's "By Due Process of Law" (1923) (*Scribner's*, April, 1923) again speaks of the divided loyalties begat by the war. In this case the Brandon family of Mississippi, having originated in Massachusetts, is loyal to the Union. In June, 1862, John, the young son of Augustine Brandon, has finished his first year at Harvard College and has made his way back to Mississippi with the purpose of securing his father's permission to enlist in the Union Army. Upon arriving at the family plantation, he meets a disturbing sight. The plantation buildings have been set afire by soldiers of a Union Calvary detachment. His father stands on the steps of the family home and is killed by a volley of bullets fired at the command of a man called "the Cossack." Young Brandon is clubbed senseless by a group of soldiers before he can rush to the scene. He wakes the next morning to find his father dead and his sister driven raving mad. Brandon takes his sister to an asylum in the North and enlists in the Union army.

The story then moves twelve years into the future, to May 30, 1874, the day before Decoration (Memorial) Day. A stranger named John visits the G. A. R. Hall of Centreville, Illinois. While interacting with the members of the post John hears one member refer to a man called Conrad as "Cossack." John, who, of course, is John Brandon, returns to Centreville on the Fifth of July. He attends the G. A. R. meeting that night with an arrest warrant and extradition papers for Max Conrad on the charge of murdering Augustine Brandon in June, 1862. Even though Brandon is accompanied by two marshals and papers signed by the governor of Illinois, there is great resistance to the idea of Conrad being tried in

Mississippi. Averting an incident, Brandon suggests that Conrad be tried there, in the G. A. R. hall, by the post. If Conrad is found not guilty, Brandon will drop his attempts at extradition. The trial ensues. Caesar, Augustine Brandon's servant, had accompanied Brandon to Centreville and testified that Augustine Brandon had offered no resistance to the Union troops. The man serving as attorney for Conrad objects to Caesar's testimony, observing that Mississippi "doesn't allow a white man to be convicted on the testimony of one old nigger."[91] Given that the proceeding was not an official court, Caesar was allowed to testify. Much to the surprise of Conrad, two other men, one a member of the post, corroborate Caesar's testimony. Conrad rises to protest, claiming that he could not be tried for acts he committed as a Union soldier. Slowly, each of the G. A. R. members vacates the hall, leaving Conrad in the custody of Brandon and the marshals. The next morning two armed and uniformed G. A. R. members stood guard as Conrad was loaded onto the train for Mississippi.

Like the earlier stories from the Civil War, Stimson's story features a romantic hero. Brandon overcomes tragedy and dishonor with the rule of law, enforced by the noble Grand Army of the Republic. In contrast to Singmaster's stories there is a clear villain who is also a member of the G. A. R. Thus, the story melds the romantic ideal with a sense of realism. "By Due Process of Law" may also be seen in the context of Burt's "The Blood Red One." Does the rule of law apply to crimes committed in wartime? Stimson's story, by applying the question to the Civil War, seems to strike an affirmative response.

The complexity of North/South relations is further dramatized later in a yarn by the superb humorist Irvin S. Cobb, "No Dam' Yankee" (*Cosmopolitan*, November, 1927) (1928). Cobb's story involves a strange triangle between the three commissioners of the Shiloh Military Park some forty years after the end of the war. An Act of Congress required that two of the three commissioners be former Union soldiers and the third be a confederate. Colonel Van Duzer, formerly of the G. A. R., and General MacAllister, formerly of the Confederate Army, were two members of the Commission, who were often at disagreement with one another. The third Commission member, and its chairman, Major Todd was a former Union soldier of southern origins. Indeed, he was a southerner in all respects, except for his allegiance to the Union. He took great pride in pointing out that, although he was a Union veteran he was not a Yankee.

Major Todd was thrust into yet another disagreement when the son of Colonel Van Duzer and the daughter of MacAllister had fallen in love and plotted to marry against their fathers' wishes. The plot involves two racing steamboats, an irate father, and a third party bearing the wedding license. Seizing upon convenience and the urgency of the moment, Major Todd facilitates the wedding ceremony, conducted by the Right Reverend Virgil K. Bogardus, D.D., of Florence, Alabama, Bishop of the Zion A. M. E. Church, District of Northern Alabama and Northern Mississippi. General MacAllister is outraged that his daughter has not only married a Yankee, but that the ceremony was conducted by a negro. He berates his colleague, telling him that the marriage would never have happened had Major Todd and others not fought to free the slaves. He was interrupted by Major Todd, who tells him to put his misgivings aside and to embrace his child and son-in-law. Todd goes on, however, to set the record straight on the other matter, reiterating that he had fought to preserve the Union and that he was not a cursed Yankee.

Todd's final comment reminds us that the nation was still highly divided on issues of race, even among those who counted themselves as victors in the American Civil War. The same theme is signaled in Stimson's story as well. The conventional milieu of the Civil War is somewhat muddied by the fact that Union soldiers raided the home of a pro-Union family in Mississippi (a family that also holds slaves). In Illinois, the GAR veterans are reluctant to accept the testimony of a "nigger." And, even as accounts of the Great War begin to hone something of a bitter edge, glorious memories of the Civil War live on.

The second phase of stories from the Great War differs from the first in its sense of involvement. Although depiction continues to be a strong motif, the drift of the stories moves away from a depiction of events to one that gives apparent meaning to the strange happenings. The story writers are more evident in their attempts to shape that meaning. Madness of the type found in the years of trench warfare cannot be simply dismissed. The move is to connect it to a spiritual purpose. Even in the jingoistic "Toast to the Forty-Five" and "Extra Men" the overt patriotism is accompanied by a strong element of civic and, in the case of Pelley's story, Christian spirituality. Things happen for a purpose. The Civil War stories seem to be attempts to return to a simpler time.

# Just the Facts

By the late twenties the tone of the war stories about the Great War begins to change. Gone are the uplifting themes and spiritual explanations. In their place have come stories that are starkly realistic and rather cynical. In the 1927 volume J. P. Marquand's "Good Morning Major," (*Saturday Evening Post*, December, 1926) addresses, for the first time, "chickenshit,"[92] the routinized harassment of lower ranking men that often characterizes the military experience. From that chickenshit comes another of the ever present ironies in the war. The story, written in the voice of a young major, begins in a training camp for new troops commanded by a regular Army veteran, General Swinnerton. The General is old-school Army, a man who earned his way to general all the way from the enlisted ranks with service in the Indians wars and the Philippines. The young officers under his command, particularly Billy Langwell, are college men who hold the General somewhat in contempt. Langwell strides around in a custom-made uniform, accessorized with silver spurs and a riding crop. He notes to the narrator that the General is not a gentleman and vows to put him in his place. The General likewise does not understand the college educated young men under his command, particularly Langwell. They take the training camp and the business of becoming soldiers as something of a lark. The general calls the Major and Langwell into his office and talks of his Army experience which started as a buck private in 1875 and included fighting Navajos on horseback and hand-to-hand combat in the Philippines. The General, himself, had attended only military schools and expected that the men under his command would be soldiers. Swinnerton tries to drill into the officers the seriousness of war. The men, however, are incapable of a connecting with the General.

The troops eventually sail for France and, upon arriving, are quickly thrust into battle. In the turmoil and confusion, communication lines are cut and the General attempts to read a map and to make sense of the French place names. Langwell cannot control his laughter as he watches the situation. General Swinnerton flies into a rage and eventually sends Langwell to headquarters, through the front lines, in the dark, under heavy shelling, to obtain the coordinates for artillery fire. It is nearly a suicide mission and most of the officers think it was retribution. Langwell arrives back severely wounded and without the coordinates. The General seeks other troops to gain information. A Lieutenant Swinnerton, who turns out to be the General's son, arrives at their command post, reporting for duty, and the General immediately orders him to pursue the same task he had given to Langwell. Langwell, lying in a stretcher, concedes to the General what an idiot he was. He understands now how the General works and sees that they are totally different kinds of people.

Eventually the General gets a call from headquarters. When he asked what has become of the last messenger he is sent he is informed of Lieutenant Swinnerton's death. The General shows a brief dash of emotion, but reins himself in and brushes off any attempts at condolences. He brusquely tells the Major to list Lieutenant Swinnerton in the morning report as killed. He dismisses the Major and retires to his quarters. Everyone has been put into his place and, as George Garrett will write in a story that appears in the series over thirty years later, only the Army wins "The Old Army Game."

William March's "Fifteen from Company K" (*Midland*, November-December, 1930) appears in 1931. This story is a pastiche of vignettes about 15 soldiers in a variety of settings that is starkly different from the ones that appeared previously. Gone is any spiritually uplifting mood. Gone, too, is any moralizing. Now, the tone is grimly matter of fact. The presentation is chaotic. The stories vary in date. Some are told as if written during the war, others are reminiscences. In some instances, as in the first rather startling story, the narration is given by dead men. In that story a patient in the gas wards, Corporal Lloyd Summerville, reports in grizzly detail all the suffering going on around him and, finally, his own death. This is contrasted by the more upbeat account of Private Terwilliger, who survives the war after having been shot through both cheeks of his mouth, with no lingering damage but a pair of dimples that become the envy of all his wife's friends. Another man, Lieutenant Edward Frankel, reports how a photo of Lillian Gish kept him alive during the war. Corporal Leslie Jourdan, a violin student before the war, tells of a chance encounter with a former musician colleague after the war. The former colleague cannot understand why Jourdan has not continued to play his instrument. Jourdan removes his hands from his pocket to display his left hand that had been destroyed by shrapnel. Private William Anderson reports of his medical treatment in a battlefield hospital, without benefit of anesthesia. A corpsman tells him that the morphine they have left is being saved for the officers. The patient threatens to write a letter to President Wilson. An exasperated doctor, bloody from treating the wounded, shouts that the corpsman should give him something to shut him up.

Sergeant Arthur Chrenshaw returns to his home town where he is celebrated with a special day in his honor. The bank president, master of ceremonies for the event, speaks of Crenshaw's valor in glowing terms. Crenshaw, whose family is not of stellar reputation, later attempts to borrow $500 to start a chicken farm and goes to the same bank president for an interview. He reports the results of the interview in a matter of fact tone. He was turned down politely, but in no uncertain terms.

Private Edward Romano tells of being alone at an observation post at night. A man approaches him, but he lowers his rifle when he sees that the man is Jesus Christ. Christ asks Romano if he would have hurt him. Romano answers affirmatively, cursing that Christ should have let the war go on like it was. Christ states that there is nothing he can do about it. Both Romano and the savior begin to weep. This story is contrasted by a scene of a return to normalcy. Private Harold Dresser was awarded the Croix de Guerre, Medal Militaire, Distinguished Service Cross, and the Medal of Honor for his wartime valor. He now lives a quiet, peaceful life and works at the General Hardware Company. Dresser's fate is then contrasted with the tale of Private Phillip Calhoun who stands in a town destroyed by an artillery barrage. All that remains standing is a solitary wall of limestone adorned with a framed painting of a crown of thorns and a bleeding heart from which emanate flames. The man marvels that this one wall has remained standing and, as he stands before it, adjusting his pack, the wall falls down, crushing him to death.

Corporal Sylvester Keith comes home from the war resolute in his opinion that war should never happen again. He organizes a group of 50 intelligent men, The Society for the Prevention of War, with which he meets every Thursday. The members are very curious about the weapons of modern warfare and express outrage at the carnage it had wrought. But, he reports, when a company of National Guard was formed in town, the members of the society joined up en masse.

Sergeant Jack Howe reports of returning from the war and being honored at a dance. A beautiful young lady at the dance is totally enamored with him, but he realizes that she would never have spoken to him if he had not been in uniform. Another Sergeant matter of factly tells of coming upon a wounded German soldier in the Argonne Forest. The German begs him for a drink of water. The Sergeant reminds the German of atrocities committed by the Germans against women and children. He then beats the man to death with his rifle butt and pours out his canteen on the lifeless body.

Corporal Howard Virtue feigns shell shock to get out of combat and is so successful that he is shipped home to an insane asylum. Unfortunately, his ruse is so successful that he is committed for life. Another soldier, Sergeant Carroll Hart, tells of how he killed a German soldier who was reaching into his uniform tunic. The man, it turns out, was not reaching for a gun, but for a picture of a little girl.

The last vignette is narrated by Private John Citron, who had found a letter on the front that had been written to Francis R. Toleman. It is a fascinating letter and he hopes Toleman will contact him. Could Toleman tell him if he and Milly ever made up?

March's vignettes portray the war with a grim reality absent in the earlier stories. They still feature the characteristic irony of many stories about the Great War, but gone is any notion of war as spiritually uplifting. Christ admits that there is nothing he can do about the war and a man is crushed to death by a wall bearing a crown of thorns. One is left with both a feeling of hopelessness and of business as usual. Life goes on, but not necessarily with purpose.

By 1932 a grim tale depicting the fate of Germany appears again. Bernhard Johan Tüting's "The Family Chronicle" (*Atlantic,* December, 1931) relates a tale of the Schulte family. Again, the tone is matter of fact, devoid of the spirituality or patriotism so prominent in earlier stories. It is near Christmas, 1918, and Rudolph Schulte takes his second cousin, Heinrich, on a tour of the family farm that will soon be passed on to him. The farm has been in the family for a thousand years and Rudolph shares with the young man knowledge that has been passed on by generations of farmers. They are also searching for a Christmas tree and Rudolph furtively hopes that Heinrich will spend Christmas with him and his wife. They talk about the weather, the cold in Russia, were the younger man had served, and eventually an issue both men had skirted is resolved. Heinrich will be going to his parents' home for Christmas. He speaks:

> The first time in four years that all of our family will be at home for the holidays—only one more week until then.
> A sudden sadness struck the old man's soul. His face grew ash-gray. Ah, Heinrich was not his son! "All of you will be together then," he said.[93]

It is now Christmas, which Herr and Frau Schulte have observed without a tree. Schulte works on a task he has put off, updating the family chronicle. The farm had been handed down from generation to generation. He reads of the family's travails in previous wars. Only one boy had survived the Seven Years War, but he had sired four sons. Rudolph records in the family chronicle the lives and deaths of his four sons:

Rudolph—Herman—Heinrich—Ernst Schulte. Fallen, World War, 1914-1918.

> Our line has come to an end. I, Rudolph Schulte, the last of Schulte, leave
> this place to Heinrich Schulte, my cousin's son.
> I curse whoever should dare to read this our history without the deepest of awe,
> and with the help of God do I curse whoever should dare to alienate our farm.
> So help me God.[94]

Schulte joins his wife in bed. "Well, Christmas is over, Katharina." "Yes it is over."[95] Indeed, for the Schulte, Christmas is over forever. The story is a profound contrast to the optimism seen in the 1918 stories addressing the wartime exploits of the Buchan's and Fullers. It also represents Germany's utter devastation.

Even while Tüting's story provides a sympathetic portrayal of Germany, American writers continue to portray ironic and romantic accounts of the Civil War. Lawrence Stallings, "Gentleman in Blue" (*Saturday Evening Post*, 20 February 1932) tells of a Virginia family, near Appomattox, visited by Union cavalry soldiers just before the surrender. The leader of the group removes his cap and, "by some trick of leg brought the horse low at his right shoulder, as he swept his cap along its withers to the ground," politely asks for fire to light their pipes.[96] The mother, impressed by the gentlemanly behavior of the man, eventually invites the whole troop into her kitchen for bread and butter. Shortly thereafter the family watches in shock as a group of Confederates pursues the troop and kills the gentlemanly officer at their front gate. The account portrays the tragedy and senselessness of war. Though told from the perspective of a Southern family it contrasts the gallant portrayal of the Gentleman in Blue with a rather negative image of the Confederate troops.

The 1937 anthology returns to the Great War, featuring two more stories, though both are concerned less with the war's action and more with its aftermath. Each signals a change in attitude toward the war. Robert Buckner's "The Man Who Won the War" (*Atlantic Monthly*, 1937) is tale about what might have been. Cast as one of those stories that will never appear in the official records (not unlike Singmaster's "Penance"), it is a story told by another while riding on a train. An American is riding the Brussels Express and strikes up a conversation with an Englishman sitting in the compartment with him. Passing the steel furnaces in the Ruhr Valley, with their flames flickering in the dark sky, the American remarks that the scene looks like Hell. The Englishman agrees. The conversation leads to a discussion of German rearmament, the League of Nations, and our narrator's assumption that America "won the war." The last remark sets up the story and the Englishman proceeds to tell the American that *he* won the war.

The Englishman, it turns out, had been a spy before the war and, having been captured and then released, was placed in charge of a British destroyer in the North Sea when the war broke out. Early in the war, in October, 1914, the Germans were poised to thrust past the Belgian troops and on to Paris. The Belgians, at the point of desperation, send a group of men to sneak past the German lines, to the coast at Nieuport, where they were to signal British ships for help. As luck would have it, they encountered a sleeping sentry and are able to signal to ship, the destroyer captained by the Bradman. Now, Bradman and his men had discovered that their vessel was carrying a crate of some 180 eighty uniforms, kilted outfits intended for the 1$^{st}$ Cameron Highlanders. Taking a boat to shore and hearing of the Belgian plight, Bradman devises a plan whereby the Belgians wear the Scottish uniforms to deceive the Germans into thinking that the British had brought in reinforcements and thus stem the German Army's progress. The ploy works and, followed by the opening of the dikes at Yser, the Germans advanced their left flank no farther for the rest of the war. Bradman was Court Martialed because of the missing uniforms and spent the rest of the war in prison.

But there is a coda to the story. Throughout their journey Bradman has carried a package on his lap and he now tells of its purpose. Three years before, Bradman returned to Nieuport, out of curiosity. By chance, he stayed in a hotel with a German named Bechtel. He and Bechtel became friendly and Bradman tells his story to Bechtel. Bechtel, it turns out was the hapless, sleeping German sentry who had been overcome by the Belgians. Bechtel declares that it was he who was responsible for losing the war. The kicker is that Bechtel has arranged that his ashes be sent Bradman with instructions that they be buried on the beach at Nieuport. Ironies continue, but the tone of those ironies has changed. No longer does the irony point to some spiritual purpose. Rather, the irony directs more to a sense of random purposelessness.

A whimsical piece by Benedict Thielen, "Lieutenant Pearson," (*Atlantic*, 1937) is reminiscent of some of the stories of the G. A. R. Pierson, a Second Lieutenant of Infantry, who never saw action during the war, was set to lead the troops in a local parade commemorating their departure for France seventeen years before. Pearson leads the parade in a French taxi cab, one of the very vehicles used to defend Paris against the Germans, down Main Street and, as he proceeds, becomes a legend in his own mind. He advances in rank to Captain, Major, Colonel, and finally to General, all in the space of three paragraphs. Passing the reviewing stand, Pearson slowly descends in rank and self-importance back to Second Lieutenant Pearson and then back to plain Frank Pearson. Finally, the war is something about which we can find humor.

The lighter tone continues in the final story about the Great War, 1940's "Your General Does Not Sleep" (*Atlantic*, May, 1940) by Emilio Lussu. The story is set in the trenches among Italian forces. General Leone, the new divisional commander appears in the lines and asks our narrator if he has ever been wounded. When the soldier replies in the negative, the General implies that he's lacking in courage. The story goes on to detail a number of episodes in which the omnipresent General seems to defy death and reason: he stands up on top of the trench and is not hit by a hail of bullets; he appears out of the darkness of at night, fully dressed, and exhorts sleepy troops to stay awake. The General orders the men into situations in which there is almost certain death. At one point the troops hear that the General has been killed in battle and they actually have a party in which they drink wine and toast his death. As the men raise their glasses in a toast, a mounted figure on horseback appears out of the woods. It is the General, still quite alive. Finally, one man plots to have the General killed. In the trenches there are holes, or keyholes, through which one may look across no man's land to the enemy lines. One particular keyhole, number 14, has had an enemy rifle permanently aimed at it throughout the war. Many soldiers have been killed as they peered through the hole. The troops often amuse themselves by holding sticks and coins in front of the hole and watch as bullets go through the small orifice and strike the target. During an inspection of the keyholes a soldier leads the General to number 14. He walks in front of the hole several times and actually peers out through the hole for several seconds. But no bullets are forthcoming. After the General leaves, the men again put targets in front of the hole and watch as they are shot away by the enemy guns.

The last six stories about the Great War offer only depiction. Even in the lighthearted stories the message seems to be one of resignation. Things happened and there is no particular reason that they happened. War is Hell and that is about all there is to say.

The 22 stories written about World War I display consistent rhetorical tendencies, each adapting to and reflecting the time in which they were written. Stories written before the United States' involvement are written in a fashion that steadfastly tries to distinguish the European war from American concerns, but still with a touching sense of pathos. The ones written after the United States' involvement display a cheerful, fantastic patriotism and a heightened sense of spirituality. All are respectful of the human struggle involved and depict the struggles as hopeful and noble, even amidst futility. Throughout the first two periods and extending into the postwar period is a spiritual element in which authors and the American public seem to struggle to find meaning and resolution in the conflict. Though not uniformly, the stories concerning spirituality tend to be first and second hand accounts of strange occurrences. They have a gospel-like quality that seems to render them in the form of sacred testimony. By 1927 the spiritual tone ends and the stories become infused with a sense of realism. The accounts they offer are neither noble nor uplifting. They present the facts with little commentary, but a lot of attitude. The stories are presented with a certain irony which reflects something of a bemused sneer.

Using the language of Burke's pentad, the early stories of the Great War feature an emphasis on scene, depicting the events from overseas at a linguistic distance. Eventually, when the U. S. is about to enter the conflict the stories place far greater emphasis on act and purpose. This produces the mystical, spiritual quality seen in stories written later in the war ("White Battalion," "The Story Vinton Heard at Mallorie," "Beyond the Cross"). The stories aimed at rallying American support for the war fuse a mystical purpose with a description of the act (see "Toast to the Forty-Five," "Extra Men"). The final, realistic stage of the stories from the Great War emphasizes act and scene over purpose. Nowhere, except for "Toast to the Forty-Five," is much emphasis placed on the agent, and there that emphasis is displaced by the story's mystical element.

Throughout the era featuring stories about the Great War, some five stories concerning the Civil War look back upon it with a certain romantic fondness. The emphasis is more on the agents in the stories than the act, scene, or purpose. Americans continue to write about war for the next 64 years, but only the Civil War continues to receive such reverence.

The omniscient narrator has the most license in rhetorical commentary, yet in most of the stories reviewed here it is used with the most moderation. The most melodramatic and fantastical piece of the lot, Pelley's "Toast to the Forty-Five," however, features the most heavy handed moralizing and speech making. Nonetheless, its subtle use in "In Berlin" and "La Derniére Mobilisation" seems the most powerful.

Second person accounts though limited, often seem to be the most rhetorically powerful. Somehow, the fact that the story is several sources removed, not unlike "urban myths," seems to remove the narrator from authorship and authority, but also to consider a thought for the sake of the idea alone. A vague, uncertain explanation is better than certain puzzlement. Like a ghost story, they seem more authentic when attributed to absent others.

First person accounts need be more authoritative to be believable. They can nonetheless carry a veracity missing in the omniscient and second hand accounts. In general, the first and second person narratives have a distinctly oral style. One imagines the voice of a story teller rather than a writer. These narratives come across as testimony, speech.

What, then, can be said of the short story as a rhetorical genre? First, echoing Foley, the short story's efficacy is highly dependent upon its audience. The deplorable scenes of the Great War presented in the early stories would not resonate as well with an audience committed to the war. Likewise, the fantastic, patriotic pieces of 1918, as well as the highly spiritual ones, seem almost laughable when read outside of their era. Interestingly, the omniscient pieces seem to better stand the test of time. Second, the short story can serve as a powerful tool of persuasion in ways that novels, books, and non-fiction prose cannot. A novel is a labor intensive effort that requires years in production. Books and non-fiction prose, by their very nature, are more transparent in nature. A short story can have a relatively quick composition and production time. Authorship can also be somewhat ignored. The characters' voices are seemingly their own, presented in the form of normal interaction and conversation. It has the potential to be both topical and timely.

Does the pattern observed in the stories from the Great War continue in World War II? As we shall see in the next section, the answer is no. Readers and writers, and the times in which they lived, are far more subtle and cynical. The age of the storyteller is over.

# Endnotes

1. Elsie Singmaster, "Survivors," in Edward J. O'Brien, ed., *The Best Short Stories of 1915 and the Yearbook of the American Short Story* (Boston: Small, Maynard and Company, 1916), 228.

2. Singmaster, "Survivors," 231.

3. Singmaster, "Survivors," 234.

4. Elsie Singmaster, "Penance," in Edward J. O'Brien, ed., *The Best Short Stories of 1917 and the Yearbook ofthe American Short Story* (Boston: Small, Maynard and Company, 1918), 263.

5. Singmaster, "Penance," 290.

6. Singmaster, "Penance," 293.

7. Will Levington Comfort, "Chautonville," in Edward J. O'Brien, ed., *The Best Short Stories of 1915 and the Yearbook of the American Short Story* (Boston: Small, Maynard and Company, 1916), 46.

8. Comfort 51.

9. Comfort 53.

10. Comfort 54.

11. W. A. Dwiggins, "La Derniére Mobilisation," in Edward J. O'Brien, ed., *The Best Short Stories of 1915 and the Yearbook of the American Short Story* (Boston: Small, Maynard and Company, 1916), 55.

12. Dwiggins 56.

13. Virgil Jordan, "Vengeance is Mine," in Edward J. O'Brien, ed., *The Best Short Stories of 1915 and the Yearbook of the American Short Story* (Boston: Small, Maynard and Company, 1916), 145.

14. Jordan 146.

15. Jordan 146.

16. Jordan 146.

17. Jordan 147.

18. Jordan 147.

19. Jordan 151.

20. Jordan 152.

21. Jordan 152.

22. Mary Boyle O'Reilly, "In Berlin," in Edward J. O'Brien, ed., *The Best Short Stories of 1915 and the Yearbook of the American Short Story* (Boston: Small, Maynard and Company, 1916), 196.

23. Fanny Kemble Johnson, "The Strange-Looking Man," in Edward J. O'Brien, ed., *The Best Short Stories of 1917 and the Yearbook of the American Short Story* (Boston: Small, Maynard and Company, 1918) , 361-62.

24. Johnson 362.

25. Johnson 363-64.

26. Johnson 364.

27. Edward J. O'Brien, ed., *The Best Short Stories of 1918 and the Yearbook of the American Short Story* (Boston: Small, Maynard and Company, 1919), 379.

28. Mary Mitchell Freedley, "Blind Vision," in Edward J. O'Brien, ed., *The Best Short Stories of 1918 and the Yearbook of the American Short Story* (Boston: Small, Maynard and Company, 1919), 85.

29. Freedley 86.

30. Freedley 87.

31. Freedley 89-90.

32. Freedley 90.

33. Freedley 90.

34. Freedley 91.

35. Freedley 91.

36. G. Humphrey, "The Father's Hand," in Edward J. O'Brien, ed., *The Best Short Stories of 1918 and the Yearbook of the American Short Story* (Boston: Small, Maynard and Company, 1919), 127.

37. Humphrey 128.

38. Humphrey 130.

39. Frances Gilchrist Wood, "The White Battalion," in Edward J. O'Brien, *The Best Short Stories of 1918 and the Yearbook of the American Short Story* (Boston: Small, Maynard and Company, 1919), 329.

40. Wood 329.

41. Wood 330.

42. Wood 330.

43. Wood 331.

44. Wood 331-32.

45. Katharine Prescott Moseley, "The Story Vinton Heard at Mallorie," in Edward J. O'Brien, ed., *The Best Short Stories of 1918 and the Yearbook of the American Short Story* (Boston: Small, Maynard and Company, 1919) 192.

46. Moseley 196.

47. Moseley 196.

48. Moseley 197.

49. Moseley 198.

50. Moseley 198.

51. Moseley 199.

52. Harrison Rhodes, "Extra Men," in Edward J. O'Brien, ed., *The Best Short Stories of 1918 and the Yearbook of the American Short Story* (Boston: Small, Maynard and Company, 1919) 223.

53. Rhodes 226.

54. Rhodes 227.

55. Rhodes 227-28.

56. Rhodes 230.

57. Rhodes 231.

58. William Dudley Pelley, "The Toast to the Forty-Five," in Edward J. O'Brien, ed., *The Best Short Stories of 1918 and the Yearbook of the American Short Story* (Boston: Small, Maynard and Company, 1919) 202.

59. Pelley 215.

60, Pelley 216.

61. Pelley 217.

62. Pelley 217.

63. Pelley 218.

64. Pelley 219.
65. Pelley 219.
66. Pelley 220.
67. Fleta Campbell Springer, "Solitaire," in Edward J. O'Brien, ed., *The Best Short Stories of 1918 and the Yearbook of the American Short Story* (Boston: Small, Maynard and Company, 1919) 257.
68. Springer 257.
69. Julian Street, "The Bird of Serbia," in Edward J. O'Brien, ed., *The Best Short Stories of 1918 and the Yearbook of the American Short Story* (Boston: Small, Maynard and Company, 1919) 269.
70. Street 281-82.
71. Street 291.
72. Street 292.
73. Maxwell Struthers Burt, "The Blood-Red One," in Edward J. O'Brien, ed., *The Best Short Stories of 1919 and the Yearbook of the American Short Story* (Boston: Small, Maynard and Company, 1920) 96.
74. Burt 101.
75. Burt 103.
76. Burt 103.
77. Burt 106.
78. Burt 106.
79. Burt 106.
80. Dana Burnett, "Beyond the Cross," in Edward J. O'Brien, ed., *The Best Short Stories of 1923 and the Yearbook of the American Short Story* (Boston: Small, Maynard and Company, 1924) 100.
81. Burnett 104.
82. Burnett 105.
83. Burnett 107.
84. Burnett 107.
85. Burnett 120.
86. Burnett 123.
87. Burnett 124.
88. Burnett 124.
89. Solon K. Stewart, "The Contract of Corporal Twing," in Edward J. O'Brien, ed., *The Best Short Stories of 1923 and the Yearbook of the American Short Story* (Boston: Small, Maynard and Company, 1924) 336.
90. Stewart 339.
91. F. J., Stimson, F. J., "By Due Process of Law," in Edward J. O'Brien, ed., *The Best Short Stories of 1923 and the Yearbook of the American Short Story* (Boston: Small, Maynard and Company, 1924) 356.
92. This is a term of art defined by Paul Fussell as follows: "Chickenshit refers rather to the behavior that makes military life worse than it needs be; petty harassment of the weak by the strong; open scrimmage for power and authority and prestige; sadism thinly disguised as necessary discipline; a constant 'paying off of old scores'; and insistence on the letter rather than the spirit of ordinances" (*Wartime: Understanding and Behavior in the Second World War* [Oxford UP, 1989, p.80]).

93. Bernard Johann Tüting, "The Family Chronicle," in Edward J. O'Brien, ed., *The Best Short Stories of 1932 and the Yearbook of the American Short Story* (New York: Dodd, Mead and Company, 1932) 247.

94. Tüting 252.

95. Tüting 252.

96. Laurence Stallings, "Gentleman in Blue," in Edward J. O'Brien, ed., *The Best Short Stories of 1932 and the Yearbook of the American Short Story* (New York: Dodd, Mead and Company, 1932) 235.

# Chapter Two:
# The World Goes to War Again

The United States again lapsed into isolationism after the Great War. As Japan occupied Manchuria and Germany rearmed and moved to occupy much of Europe, America was mired in the problems of the Great Depression. Popular culture provided a fine distraction. Americans were listening to Jeanette MacDonald and Nelson Eddy sing "Indian Love Call," Fred Astaire voice "A Fine Romance," and Bing Crosby croon "Pennies from Heaven" in 1936. On the screen in 1937 they delighted to "Snow White and the Seven Dwarves," "Broadway Melody of 1938," and "The Awful Truth." 1938 heard Artie Shaw and his orchestra play "Begin the Beguine," Ella Fitzgerald singing "A-Tisket, A-Tasket," and the Andrews Sisters' "Bei Mir Bist Du Schoen." By 1939 film audiences were viewing "The Wizard of Oz," "Mr. Smith Goes to Washington," and another Civil War epic, "Gone With the Wind." Nonetheless, even as the stories of World War I continue into 1940, precursors to World War II are already being published. The first wave comes in a series of stories about the Spanish Civil War. The second involves the situation in Europe as German troops begin to occupy much of the continent. Finally, the impact of the new war is felt in the United States as refugees from Europe become a part of American life. Like the early stories of the Great War these stories begin transitioning the war into an American concern. And, again, like the early stories from the Great War, they utilize rhetorical depiction to suggest to their readers that something must be done. The devastation depicted features the impact on people, families, and their relations to each other.

The Spanish Civil war had already been memorialized in Picasso's "Guernica," which was initially displayed at the World's Fair in Paris in 1937. That painting portrayed the devastation of the small town of Guernica by German warplanes brought into the conflict by Fascist/Nationalist forces. The Spanish War is the venue for two stories, Prudencio de Pereda's "The Spaniard" (1939;

*Story*, 1938) and Ernest Hemingway's "Under the Ridge' (1940; *Cosmopolitan*, October 1939). Both stories highlight the divided loyalties the war inserts into the world, a country, a family, and humanity in general. The first story involves two cousins, one Spanish, Lito, and the other American-born, Domingo—known as Mickey. The American is visiting Spain during the time of the war. His cousin, Lito, has been fighting with the Nationalists (Fascists) and returns from the front with a badly injured arm. Mickey, who narrates the story, is sympathetic to the Republican troops. Mickey is staying with his cousin's family and does everything he can to avoid contact with his cousin. His very presence in the household causes a great deal of tension. Eventually, Mickey goes to visit Lito, whose injuries have now required him to stay in bed. Lito tells Mickey that he is dying. Unfortunately, their discussion leads to talk of the war. Lito claims to have "taken" one of the Republican women and this further estranges the two cousins. Mickey asks Lito if he really did it. Lito brags: "'I got one. She took me. She knew that it was the firing squad or me." He laughed a little. 'That's part of all this boy.'"[1] The remark and the satisfied look on Lito's face enrages Mickey and he grabs a straight razor from a nearby table and holds it against his cousin's throat: "This is for that girl. I just press down the blade and she will be all right again. . . . . Eh, Lito? Do I kill you? Do I kill you justly or am I still a Spaniard?"[2] Mickey drops the razor and leaves the room

Eventually, Lito nears his final days and asks that Mickey come to his room once more. This time Mickey tells him the truth about the Republican girl. There was no rape:

> "Mickey, that girl—"All during that time the girl; and how weak his voice was. "It wasn't that way. She let me. She wanted me. I found her out on the road alone. . . . She would never have seen me, Mickey . . . . But I went up to where she could see me and we challenged each other. . . . We began to talk, then. I made a little joke, you know, about how pretty she was. She laughed. 'You are still a little bit like a Spaniard, eh?' she said to me." He laughed a little. "'I am all a Spaniard,' I said. Then I threw my gun down, and I walked right over to her. She put her gun down and stayed there looking at me. She was very beautiful. I kissed her and she put her arms around my neck."
>
> "I made love to her. It was wonderful, Mickito. And then afterward, after that, I showed her the way back. . . . I know she got back because afterward I heard someone yell and then laughing.
>
> Two of our men came then. I told of all wrongly about the section. Then, when the rest came, we hit another part and they were all set in that place. I hurt my arm there. That's all. That's the way it is."[3]

Mickey does not want to look at his cousin. After a moment, Lito continued: "I wanted to—I wanted to tell it to you in an angry, hard voice. Yell it! What you said made me mad. About the little frightened girls, you know. I'm a Spaniard. I'm a Spaniard, too."[4] And then he holds Mickey's hand until he dies.

Pereda's story shows a clear connection between the United States and the nascent war in Europe. It is becoming apparent that America can no longer stand aside and hope not to be involved. There is no editorializing in the story. Rather, the depiction of the tense, unfortunate, situation presents a picture that is worth a thousand additional words.

Hemingway's "Under the Ridge" portrays some of the same conflicts. The story features the narrator, a writer of newsreels and the newsreel cameraman on the lines with Republican forces. They stop at a command post in a cave. The forces there are an international group of Hungarians, Russians, Poles, North Americans, and French, along with some Spanish soldiers. Though presumably united in a common cause, the international forces are divided by ancient animosities. A Spanish soldier, who identifies himself with the Extremadura region of Spain, tells the newsmen that he despises all foreigners and asks them if they are Russians. The Extremaduran, who is quite antagonistic, is asked by the reporter of his home town. He replies that he is from Badajoz. Badajoz, he says had been previously sacked and pillaged English, French, and Moors. He says that English forces had burned his family home and killed his grandmother. By this time the narrator is on the defensive. He expresses regret for the man's family tragedy and goes on to ask why the man harbors hatred for Americans. His father, it turns out, had been drafted to serve in Cuba and was killed by American forces there. Again expressing regrets, the reporter asks the man why he hates Russians. Russians, the Extremaduran says, represent tyranny.

After this conversation the newsmen are approached by a pair of soldiers seeking a Frenchman, who has decided to desert. They watch as the men see the man they are looking for and pursue him like hounds," shooting at the man repeatedly with pistols. The Frenchman had tired of the stupidity of the war and had simply walked away, a sentiment with which the narrator identifies. Even though the Frenchman had walked away to certain death, the narrator feels that he had preserved his dignity.

A conversation followed with the Extramaduran about the discipline that is necessary in a time of war. The Extramaduran tells of the story of a boy, Paco, from his own province. Paco had shot himself in the hand to get out of battle. His wound eventually necessitated the amputation of his hand. When he had healed other soldiers brought him back to the front and shot him at the site of the battle from which he had run. The man who shot the young soldier, in the back, was a Russian who spoke very poor Spanish.

The narrator, the newsman, understands it is time to leave this place. The Extramaduran asks him if he understands his hatred and he responds that he does. The Extramaduran extends his hand for a handshake and wishes them luck. They left the scene and, as the writer writes about it some months later, he concludes that the only winner in the situation they had witnessed was the Frenchman, though triumph was very brief. Again, we are left with a very powerful picture. Even though the narrator can comprehend the situation, the situation remains. It is inescapable.

Clearly, there is a tension building up across Europe. That tension is the scene that foments war and sets people against each other. Hemingway's story closes with explicit understanding among the participants that enormous pressure has been created by concerns beyond their control. The participants not only understand it, but accept it. Its seeds certainly were sown in the Great War, but, as this story shows, American complicity can be seen as far back as the Spanish-American War. Meanwhile, Germany is on the move.

By 1940 American popular culture had begun to reflect a greater concern with world affairs. Charlie Chaplin produced and starred in "The Great Dictator" in 1940, a parody of Adolph Hitler. Though popular song continued to be escapist with popular hits like Glenn Miller's "Chattanooga Choo Choo," Tommy Dorsey's Orchestra, with vocalist Frank Sinatra, scored a success with "I'll Never Smile Again." Dorsey's song was particularly popular in Great Britain. Winston Churchill brought tears to Sinatra's eyes years later when he told him that the song had helped keep hope alive for Londoners during the blitz.[5]

Kay Boyle's "Anschluss" (1940; *Harper's*, April, 1939) presents another chilling scene of the unfolding events in Europe. Merrill, an American fashion editor's assistant stationed in Paris, has traveled to Brenau, Austria, for a semi-annual vacation she has regularly taken for a number of years. There she will visit her friend, Toni, and his sister, Fanni. Year after year they have frolicked together in the winter snow and summer sun. When she first met the siblings Toni had just been released from prison for political activities. He was arrested again during one of her previous visits for political agitation, in Merrill's words, or what Fanni describes as treason. The matter is treated lightly and Toni plays harmonica for the women from his cell window. Merrill begs Toni to leave the country and join her in Paris. Toni declares that he must stay in his country and kisses her, smearing lipstick, rouge, and mascara all over her face. She protests that he now has red smeared all over his face. He declares that he will never wash it off.

For this visit, however, things have changed. German troops have now occupied Austria, and Merrill wonders how the change will affect Toni. She muses that Toni will never give in. He will continue to protest against the Nazis just as he had protested against all the other groups that had been in power. On this Summer day no one meets her at the station. She sees the hotels in the distance with banners bearing swastikas fluttering in the breeze. A porter eventually greets her with a snappy "Heil Hitler."

She goes to the lake, where Toni is a Sports Organizer. The bathhouses on the lake are likewise adorned with swastikas. The lake is busy with activity, full of German tourists. Toni greets Merrill, critically, at the water, where she has worn a two-piece bathing suit. Her bathing attire and her lacquered nails offend his new found sense of propriety. When Merrill comments on how the country has changed, Toni lectures her on how Austria is no longer a playground for English and Americans. The Germans, he says, respect Austria as a country. Merrill only sees Toni once again, when she leaves the train station for Paris. Across the platform she sees Toni waiting, in uniform, with other men, for another train. She sees Toni's hand and lips move from across the platform, but is unsure whether he has bid her a farewell or a "Heil Hitler." Here, before the swastika becomes the international symbol for total depravity, Boyle's account provides a chilling foreshadowing of what is to come. Again, the scenic, material concerns outweigh the personal.

David Cornell DeJong's "That Frozen Hour" (1942; *Harper's Bazaar*, May 1941) is set in Daverdam, the Netherlands, in January 1940. The winter is so cold that the clock of the cathedral is permanently frozen at three o'clock. The people of the city await the winter to come to an end, and for the inevitable invasion of the Germans. Katrien has gone skating with Hans, a German boyfriend of whom the entire family disapproves. As the couple skate along the canal they squabble about their rate of speed and styles of skating. Hans embraces the girl and tries to force a kiss. Katrien struggles to get away and, as Hans persists, she pushes and claws him away: "Not from you, you dirty Nazi!" Hans replies back in stereotypical form:

> All these months you've been trying to make a fool of me. You and your whole damned and degenerate country. . . . You'll all be sorry. Soon we'll have you all where we want you! Now I'm glad I can help my country and my leader to conquer your miserable race. I'm glad that I spied on you . . . . [6]

Katrien runs away to safety.

The next scene occurs in May. Katrien and her grandmother watch from the courtyard of their house as German airplanes roar overhead and began to drop paratroopers. One of the paratroopers is about to land on their house and Katrien stands there, armed with an axe to kill him. The grandmother takes the axe away and kills the man herself. Soon, their Jewish neighbors, the Abrahams, appear at the door seeking shelter from the Nazis. When the grandmother returns to the courtyard to dispose of the body, two Jewish prostitutes, who live nearby appear. They have watched the events unfold and are fearful that the Nazis will blame it on them. The women ask the prostitutes to help as they dispose of the body in an old well. Eventually, the old Jewish couple also help. Joined by their common complicity and fear, they all swear to keep the event secret.

The plight of the Dutch people was quite a popular cause in the United States in the early forties. Dirk van der Heide's *My Sister and I: The Diary of a Dutch Boy Refugee* , translated by Mrs. Anton Deventer, sold 56,000 copies in 1941. The book portrayed the struggle of a young boy and his sister after the death of his mother in the bombing of Rotterdam. This book was later shown to be a propaganda hoax.[7]

Joan Vatsek's "The Bees" (1942; *Story*, March-April, 1941) takes us to a group of nuns displaced from their bombed out convent. They have taken refuge in a nearby farm house since the bombing. Provisions have now run out and it is time for them to go to the city. Each of the sisters feels at odds with their usual routine. As they prepare for their move they think of the beehives at their old convent. The trip back to the convent is an emotional journey, but they arrive at the hives and busy themselves with the work necessary to prepare the hives for

winter. The task was completed in two hours. The sisters enjoyed working together again: "They had enjoyed the communion of working together. They felt
restored. The little sisterhood breathed again as a unit."[8] The act is one of completion. Mother Gervaise declares: "Now we can go . . . . They knew she did not
mean that they could return to the farm."[9] Assured that the bees will survive the
winter, Mother Gervaise holds out her arms to the other sisters "enfolding them
and the beehives behind them, in a gesture of completion . . . ." "Yes," another
sister exclaims, "We will live through the winter." They all run from the field
together, laughing, "running from the past, to the busy and immediate present."[10]

Emily Hahn's "It Never Happened" (1945; New Yorker,1944) is set in Hong
Kong at the time of the Japanese invasion in 1941. The story is told by an unnamed friend about her friend, Mercedes, a Manese, a Portuguese of broadly
mixed races from Macao, a nearby Portuguese possession. Mercedes is a beautiful young woman, pursued by many suitors before the war. At the time the Japanese occupy Hong Kong Mercedes is working as a nurse in a hospital. It is
known that the soldiers were brutal to the women there. Our narrator asks Mercedes about it, trying to determine whether she had been raped. Mercedes says,
no, that she was able to hide away under a cot.

Mercedes comes to her friend once again and tells her of a plan to sneak into China across the Indochinese border with a Russian, Boris, whom she intends
to marry. The plan ultimately fails because Mercedes, an incorrigible flirt,
strikes up a relationship with Chowda, an Indian who turns out to be a Japanese
spy. Chowda turns Mercedes in to the Japanese and Boris, not yet her husband,
does escape to China. Mercedes is jailed by the Japanese, but is eventually released. The time in jail has traumatized her and one of her captors still visits her
at her home. She visits her friend again and tells her of her latest troubles. This
time Mercedes looks messy, her hair unkempt. She tells her friend of the continued harassment. Her friend attempts to comfort her in the only way the van-
quished can. The man will probably be transferred soon, she tells her and, be-
sides, she reminds her, she was able to escape from the Japanese before. Yes,
Mercedes replies with a frightened stare, telling her the story she had told before, but with greater, telling detail, indicating that the soldiers had found all the
girls, even those who were hiding. At this point the narrator knows the truth of
the story. Again she tries to comfort Mercedes, telling her that if a one puts
something out of their mind that it never occurred. Hahn was the longtime Asia
correspondent for the New Yorker. Her story no doubt had added veracity for her
regular readers. Mercedes represents many war torn persons and the countries
they called home. They are proud at first, but, ultimately, war humiliates us all.

Vahan Krikorian Gregory's "Athens, Greece, 1942" (1953; Armenian Review, 1952) portrays one desperate day in the life of fifteen year old Ara, a "thin,
young, Armenian boy" who has set out to make his daily 70 kilometer bicycle
ride away from town to exchange silk stockings for raisins, one of the few food
products available for exchange. As he rides out of town he passes the dead
body of a young girl with whom he had shared moments of intimacy three nights

earlier, in exchange for a raisin. Her death is accepted matter of factly; his family has subsisted on a few raisins and almonds a day for weeks. Ara's thoughts are totally fatalistic. He assumes that "Each member of his family would die slowly within the next few weeks."[11]

The farmer, from whom he has purchased raisins before, reluctantly gives him two handfuls of raisins for the silk stockings. The boy then rides to the sea coast in search of crabs, or fish. After a futile hour of searching, the starving boy consumes both handfuls of his raisins, only to vomit them up a few minutes later. He rides back to the farmer and offers his shoes for a fish. The farmer refuses, but grudgingly accepts the shoes for two more handfuls of raisins. The boy pedals back home, barefooted. He passes a German convoy along the way and Ara vows to throw himself beneath their wheels. He loses his nerve. The story ends with no hint as to Ara's fate. The reader can only conclude that his life continued in the miserable circumstances presented in the story.

Nancy Hales "Those are as Brothers" (1942; *Mademoiselle*, May, 1941) moves to the domestic front in the United State. Four people, each with their own issues, become acquaintances in a small neighborhood of the Connecticut Valley. A Jewish gardener, Loeb, of the nearby estate, a refugee from the concentration camps, passes time with the German governess of Mrs. Mason. The two Germans, united with a common language and hatred of the Nazis, are also divided by religion and social class. Mrs. Mason, who is divorced from a husband who brutalized her, is visited from time to time by Mr. Worthington, a young man who has romantic intentions. Mrs. Mason, however, is traumatized by her relationship with her ex-husband and cannot requite Mr. Worthington's love. Mrs. Mason is consumed by her perceived connection with the affairs in Europe. She feels that her ex-husband had been, in microcosm, like the Nazis in Germany.

The four later gathered together for a birthday of one of the Mason children. Talk inevitably turns to the war and conditions in Europe. Worthington says to Loeb: "Those concentration camps now. Just the fellows on top doing it to the fellows on the underneath . . . . it must have been a job keeping your courage up." Mr. Loeb replies that he did not maintain his courage. As the conversation continues awkwardly, Mr. Loeb attempts to speak in broad terms:

> The more and more that are pressed all the time, the more there are who know together the same thing, who have it together. When it is time and something happens to make it possible, there is something that all these people have had together and that will make them fight together. And now Frenchman, too, Belgian, too, Flemings. If you have been in a concentration camp, it is more together than that you might be of different countries.

"They remember all the same thing together," says Mrs. Mason. "Yes," Loeb replies."[12]

Later in the summer, Mr. Loeb's employer returns to her estate and starts threatening and bullying the man. She says that she will report him to the refu-

gee committee. The group of friends is outraged by the turn of events, but somehow Mrs. Mason finds courage. She says she will talk to his employer and she
will write a letter to the refugee committee. Mr. Loeb thanks her: "She smiled at
him. The tension had gone away from his eyes, the look of fear that she recognized had gone."[13]

Neither courage nor compassion saves the day in Hollywood. In Budd Wilson Schulberg's "The Real Viennese Schmaltz" (1942; *Esquire*, 1941) Hollywood studio executives have hired Hannes Dreher, an Austrian, to write a
screenplay for a Jennette MacDonald and Nelson Eddy film, "The Blue Danube." Dreher works for days on a screenplay, but produces nothing. Finally,
Dreher is given an ultimatum to produce, or lose his job. Dreher works all night
to produce a manuscript the size of the telephone book.

The producer reads the first 50 pages of the screenplay immediately and
then summons Dreher to his office: "It's got no life, no charm. It reads like a
horror story. It doesn't sound like you have ever been to Vienna."[14] Dreher is
summarily dismissed. As Dreher leaves the studio he hears the sounds of Jeanette MacDonald singing the test tracks of the score for "The Blue Danube."
The sound plunges him into a daydream. He was back in Vienna on a beautiful
Spring day. He was celebrating the completion of his new play. *The Blue Danube* was playing on the radio:

> Suddenly, in a nightmare, they were listening to the voice of Chancellor
> Schussnigg. *This day has placed us in a tragic and decisive situation . . . the
> German government . . . ultimatum . . . we have yielded to force . . . God pro-
> tect Austria!*
> *The thunder of Nazi throats and Nazi boots along the cobblestones . . . the last
> night . . . full of hoarse screams futile cries the death-rattle of old Vienna . . .
> and there was Lothar, my only son [. . .] whispering: They are hunting every
> leader of our Fatherland Front . . . I must get out [ . . . ] Then the last hope for
> freedom, the steamer anchored in the Danube ready to sail for Prague . . . Re-
> membering: the small boat the muffled oars the friendly Danube the beautiful
> blue Danube where Lothar learned to swim . . .then the angry putt-putt-putt-
> putt of the motorboat full of the cruel young faces of Lothar's classmates and
> Lothar slipping over into the dark water [. . .] the sound of steel winging along
> the surface like ducks . . . the grotesque pizzicato of the bullets plunk-plunk-
> plunking into the river . . ."*[15]

Harold Edson Brown, veteran Hollywood hack, is brought in to rehabilitate
Dreher's script. He reads through Dreher's manuscript, "feeling every second of
Dreher's last night in Austria." The script is so powerful that it "reached the
evaporating pool of integrity buried within [Brown]."[16] But, when he finishes
the manuscript, he drops it into his desk drawer. "He wondered if he was going
to let it lie buried there forever. One of these days (maybe), when he couldn't
look his fat check in the face any more, he was going to pull it out and fight for
it and watch it blast his piddling little comedies off the screen."[17] Meanwhile,
Hannes Dreher walked off of a bus "wondering how to tell his family that the

money they were waiting for to buy their way out of Vienna might not be coming for a long, long time."[18]

Vicki Baum's "This Healthy Life" (1943; *Story*, September-October, 1942) is another story about refugees, this time on an American chicken farm. Clarissa was an actress in Germany and her husband, Paul Van Porten, an Austrian Baron. They are housed at the farm of Mr. Gibbs, "whom the Society for the Settlement of European Refugees had entrusted with the thorny task of converting useless, unwanted intellectuals into useful producers of eggs."[19]

After a day of cleaning chicken coops and processing eggs, Mr. Van Porten has gone to bed. Clarissa has stayed up late talking with Mr. Lindner, a former art historian, who had seen Clarissa on stage and screen many times before the war. When Clarissa finally retires she fumbles through their cramped, dimly lit room for her mirror. Mr. Van Porten is trying to sleep and Clarissa wants him to hold the mirror for her. Van Porten holds the mirror and Clarissa starts to laugh at him: "You, in those idiotic woolies. Sears Roebucks pajamas! The farmer's delight!" Van Porten replies: "But you don't know how funny you are. You, with your forty-five years and your goddamned schoolgirl complexion and the cream smeared all over you. Sitting all night in the dark with that Jewish fellow and listening to his tirades and making eyes at him." Clarissa continues to laugh and the tired, infuriated Van Porten grabs the mirror and smashes it on the floor. The silver framed mirror was a gift from friends, commemorating Clarissa's career. Van Porten continues to rant: "Damn your mirror. Damn your friends."[20] Van Porten is suddenly contrite and stoops to help her pick up the glass," looking every year of her age. "Oh Paul, darling! She said, and began to laugh again, "Oh my darling—you should not have done it. You should not have come with me. You should have stayed over there—where you belong."[21] The closing underscores the plight of the refugee: they belong nowhere. Their lives have been disrupted and are in a constant state of unease.

The uneasiness is also present among citizens. Warren Beck's "Boundary Line" (1943; *Rocky Mountain Review*, Winter, 1942) involves a dispute between neighbors, the Giffords and the Schwartzes. The Schwartzes, a working class family of distant German heritage, are perceived by the Giffords (Mr. Gifford is a lawyer) to be surly. Once, Mr. Schwartz had asked to buy a strip of the Gifford's property in order to extend his garden, which the family tends with incredible energy. Gifford had refused. There was a later disagreement when the Schwartz children had repeatedly thrown a ball into the Gifford's garden. Following that incident the two families had stopped talking. Eventually, the Giffords had allowed their hedge to grow up so that they could no longer see their neighbors. When Germany had annexed Poland the Giffords began to think that the Schwartzes were cheered by the German advance. The couple is smug in their disdain, as they discuss the situation without irony:

"The Schwartzes are the kind of people out of whom Nazis could be made, aren't they?"

"My dear, they are Nazis," Mr. Gifford declared. "They show how Nazis come to be. Anybody is a Nazi—potential at all times, active when he gets a chance to be—who lacks the satisfactions of intelligent self-possession, and a resultant serenity and cordiality. Such fellows have to get themselves regimented to compensate for their confusion, and for their sense of inferiority insofar as they become conscious of others who are livelier and more urbane. We've had an outbreak of this morbid Germanism on the average of once a generation for four generations, my dear, and as I see it, the causes are no so much economic or political as psychological—psychopathic, in fact. The modern Germans—at least the ones who start the wars—can't stand the strain on *amour proper* of being outdistanced in the art of living by other nationalities. Their egoism and aloofness and solemn asininity are over-compensations. . . . But since they can't be lively like the French, or poised like the English, they've determined to make the best—or the worst—of what they are, and to repudiate what they can't or won't become, and their method, the Nazi method, is a pathological symptom of maladjustment—they try to creep back into the womb of the race and the state.[22]

Mrs. Gifford, without irony, agrees that he has summed up the German character precisely.

When Germany moves to annex Norway and Holland, the Giffords become even more suspicious of their neighbors. It seems that many cars have begun to come and go to the Schwartz home. Both Mr. and Mrs. Gifford begin to record the license plate numbers of the visiting cars. One night, dressed in dark clothing, Mr. Gifford goes so far as to sneak through the hedge and spy on the Schwartzes. The intelligence he offers Mrs. Gifford upon his return is that the men were playing cards and drinking beer. Unabashed, the Giffords vow to continue to record the license numbers. They agree it was good that they never sold them the strip of land. Already, before the U. S. war effort has begun fully, there is an awareness that Nazism may not only be a German phenomenon.

By 1942, the United States was fully immersed in the war. Stories were still being written about the plight abroad, however, even as Americans began to fight against Germany and Japan. Dorothy Canfield's "The Knot Hole" (1944; *Yale Review*, Spring, 1943) considers the plight of the French by means of a convention, so popular during the Great War, of recounting a story originally told by another. A group of 40 French prisoners have been confined by the Germans in a boxcar. For four months they have been told that they are being shipped back to France. The men must take turns sleeping because there is not enough room in the car for them all to recline at one time. Four buckets handle the "sanitary" needs of the men. Each man receives two cups of water per day. The outside world is seen only through cracks in the wall that allow for a sense of day and night. One day, a knot works its way free from the siding and the men are now capable of peering out of the boxcar. They agree that the track they are now waiting on is somewhere in France. Upon seeing their homeland, the men break out in song: "Amour sacré de la patrie."[23] The guards quickly silence them. For the next days they take turns looking out at the world through their hole: an old woman pushing a wheelbarrow, five school children walking along the track, a working man carrying a shovel to dig potatoes. The potato digger returns and the prisoners are convinced that every move he makes is a signal to them. The next day, while the guards are engaged in a squabble over a card game, the potato digger rushes to the car. The prisoners push a note out through the boxcar. "French," it asked. The man quickly scribbles a note in response: "Courage, Faith, Hope."[24] The prisoners reply again: "Never give up." The man returns to his spot in the field and holds his hand over his heart. Over the course of the next couple of days dozens of townspeople pass by the train, each silently holding their hands over their hearts. The prisoners are elated. At midnight, however, a guard opens the door, counts the men, and proceeds to read to the men the note they had passed to the potato digger. The guard indicates that there will be reprisals. The prisoners anxiously respond: "We were being sent back. We were being sent back to prison. We were being sent back to Germany."[25] One man screams in anguish and is immediately silenced by their leader: "Order! No screaming. We are men! . . . We have pledged ourselves to . . . We gave them our promise. They promised us . . . ." He struggles with his breath and emotions. "When he spoke again, his voice was under control. 'We have been home,' he said. 'We have been home to France. We have made a promise to France.'"[26]

The prewar stories provide an excellent transition to the stories portraying America's involvement in the war. The mood of the country is far worldlier than in the previous war. The stories now show recognition of our interconnection with world affairs. Save for "Boundary Line" and "The Knot Hole," stories that appear at about the time the United States enters the war, the stories feature no editorializing. Rather, they depict a world climate that signals to the reader the necessity of America's involvement in the war. The latter two stories move into the oratorical mode we saw in the Great War, where the writers seem to use their stories as an excuse to make a speech. Though the tone of the stories changes with America's entry into the war, the focus on the domestic front continues. The stories about the growing world war display a clear awareness of what is happening abroad and how people are being affected by warfare. Though American writers were aware of concentration camps early in the war, the particular horrors are not addressed until 42 years after the war's end. We read of the valorous resistance by ordinary people drawn into a harsh conflict and we see the portrayal of Germans begin to transform into the evil, calculating stereotype so evident in many movies about World War II. The role of the agent in these stories is again diminished. Virtually all characters are swept up in the overwhelming influence of the scene. It is a trend that continues well beyond the Second World War.

# Endnotes

1. Prudencio De Pereda, "The Spaniard," in Edward O'Brien, ed., The *Best Short Stories of 1939 and the yearbook of the American Short Story* (Boston: Houghton Mifflin, 1938), p. 213.

2. De Pereda 214

3. De Pereda 216.

4. De Pereda 217.

5. Peter J. Levinson, *Tommy Dorsey: Livin' in a Great Big Way: A Biography* (Cambridge, MA: Da Capo Press, 2005) p. 123.

6. David DeJong, "That Frozen Hour," in Martha Foley, ed., *Best American Short Stories, 1942, and Yearbook of the American Short Story* (Boston: Houghton Mifflin, 1942) 81.

7. See Fussell, *Wartime*, p. 166 and in "Writing in Wartime: The Uses of Innocence," in *Thank God for the Atom Bomb and Other Essays* (New York: Summit Books, 1988) 53-81. I have personally viewed a copy of *My Sister and I* from the University of Iowa library. The "Date Due" slip indicated it was highly read in 1941-42, but not again until my colleague, David Snowball, borrowed it in 1987.

8. Joan Vatsek, "The Bees," in Martha Foley, ed., *Best American Short Stories, 1942, and Yearbook of the American Short Story* (Boston: Houghton Mifflin,1942, 383.

9. Vatsek 384.

10. Vatsek 384.

11. Vahan Krikorian. Gregory, "Athens, Greece, 1942." in Martha Foley, ed., *Best American Short Stories, 1953, and Yearbook of the American Short Story* (Boston: Houghton Mifflin, 1953) 153.

12. Nancy Hale, "Those are as Brothers," in Martha Foley, ed., *Best American Short Stories, 1942, and Yearbook of the American Short Story* (Boston: Houghton Mifflin, 1942) 137.

13. Hale 140.

14. Budd Wilson Schulberg, "The Real Viennese Schmaltz," in Martha Foley, ed., *Best American Short Stories, 1942, and Yearbook of the American Short Story* (Boston: Houghton Mifflin, 1942) 266.

15. Schulberg 266.

16. Schulberg 267.

17. Schulberg 268.

18. Schulberg 268.

19. Vicki Baum, "This Healthy Life." in Martha Foley, ed., *Best American Short Stories, 1943, and Yearbook of the American Short Story* (Boston: Houghton Mifflin, 1943) 2.

20. Baum 9.

21. Baum 9.

22. Warren Beck, "Boundary Line," in Martha Foley, ed., *Best American Short Stories, 1943, and Yearbook of the American Short Story* (Boston: Houghton Mifflin, 1943) 18.

23. Dorothy Canfield, "The Knot Hole." in Martha Foley, ed., *Best American Short Stories, 1944, and Yearbook of the American Short Story* (Boston: Houghton Mifflin, 1944) 42.

24. Canfield 58.

25. Canfield 61.

26. Canfield 61.

# Chapter Three:
# America and the Second World War

While the stories about the Great War focused almost exclusively on the horrors and rigors of war, those in regard to World War II focused almost exclusively on the home front. While some of the stories from both wars are clearly intended to bolster the war effort, they too are different types. The stories from the Great War tend to focus on American pride, to highlight a feeling of patriotism, and of good versus evil, while the stories of World War II tend to speak much more to the paranoia that war can engender. While the stories of World War I tend to be rather explicit in presenting details, the stories of World War II are much more implicit. Absent from the stories of the Great War are any references to divided loyalties of many of immigrant Americans. Those issues are clearly present in the stories of the Second World War, though they are silent on the issue of Japanese internment until 1971. The stories of World War II do not necessarily portray the war in it noblest light. Rather, they portray a war, like any other, that must be endured by normal people trying to live from day to day The stories of World War II have a profound sensitivity to domestic issues. For the first time in the series we hear the voices of women and their testimony as to the devastating impact war has on their lives.

Popular music began referring to the war in late 1941 with titles like "Remember Pearl Harbor," "Goodbye Mama, I'm Off to Yokohama," and "Kiss the Boys Goodbye" along with Glenn Miller's "Chattanooga Choo Choo." Filmgoers saw mixed portrayals about war in a version of George Bernard Shaw's "Major Barbara" and the lionization of "Sergeant York," the American hero of the Great War, along with "Dumbo," "Citizen Kane," and "The Maltese Falcon." "Sun Valley Serenade," starring the Glenn Miller Orchestra, featured a plot about a Norwegian refugee, played by Sonja Henie. 1942 heard songs such as "He Wears a Pair of Silver Wings," "Somebody Else is Taking My Place," and Irving Berlin's "This is the Army, Mr. Jones." Donald Duck had joined the war effort in with "Donald Duck in Nutziland" (later called "Der Fuehrer's Face") which featured a popular parody song covered by Spike Jones, and a series of six shorts about the war effort from 1942-44. By 1943-44 the war had become a staple of Hollywood films with titles such as "This is the Army," "Thirty Seconds Over Tokyo," "Since You Went Away," "Stage Door Canteen," "Casablanca," and "We Dive at Dawn." Popular song titles included "When the Lights Go On Again (All Over the World)," "Comin' in on a Wing and a Prayer," "A Hot Time in the Town of Berlin," and the morale booster, "Ac-cent-tchu-ate the Positive."

Specific stories in regard to the United States' involvement in the war do not start until the 1943 volume, with most stories appearing in 1944-45. Stories about the war continue into the early fifties. Although none of the stories presents outright opposition to the war, many feature depiction of scenes which clearly focus on the down side of the war. The writings of Studs Terkel and Tom Brokaw notwithstanding, the people who lived through the war and wrote about it, the so-called "Greatest Generation," do not necessarily portray "the good war." Rather, they portray a war, like any other, that must be endured.

A few stories, particularly those by Irwin Shaw, express rather pointed observations about the war in the dialogue. Shaw, already serving in the army when the 1943 volume was published, and to whom it is dedicated, portrays the frustrations and angst of a father who has just sent his son off to war in "Preach on the Dusty Roads" (*New Yorker*, 1942). Nelson Weaver has made quite a living as a corporate accountant and now muses on the futility of his profession and on the failures and frustrations of a generation in a story that builds up to a final passage that amounts to a confession. His thoughts are articulated as an unuttered speech in which he notes that he and Hitler are of about the same age. He rues the fact that he had done nothing to stop a second world war. While the seeds of war were being sown the world over, he had worried himself with the task of earning and counting money. Now he feels guilty to be sending his son out to fight a war that he should have prevented. This story is the first of four wartime stories by Shaw included in the series. It sets the tone for a variety of stories about the war. Each portrays a different, yet powerful, narrative.

Saul Bellow's "Notes of a Dangling Man" (1944; *Partisan Review*, September-October, 1943) recounts the travails of a man tied up in the red tape of the Selective Service Agency. Called up some seven months earlier to be inducted into the army, our narrator, Joseph, has quit his job and is being supported by his wife. His initial induction date was postponed because, as a Canadian national, a background investigation was required before induction. The investigation was completed satisfactorily, but sufficient time has passed since his initial physical that a second blood test was required. The blood is fine, but a change in regulations has dictated that married men are reclassified 3A. A week later he was notified that married men were now being taken. Of course, his previous blood test had expired and so he was summoned for a new blood test. Now, reclassified as 1A, he waits. He cannot work because no one will hire men who are 1A. The tension has worn on Joseph and caused him particular problems in relating to friends and family.

Two stories portray the plight of soldiers' wives, awaiting their husband's overseas assignments: Berry Fleming's "Strike Up the Stirring Music" (1944; *Yale Review*, Summer, 1943) and Josephine W. Johnson's "The Rented Room" (1944; *Harper's Bazaar*, June, 1943) Fleming's story focuses on the wife of a young army officer living near a training camp in Georgia. The whole army thing has come as a surprise to her. She had found out only after they had been married for a year that her husband was an officer in the army reserves (He refers to the fact rather cavalierly as "a wild oat from his college days").[1] Now, as an army wife, she is gradually learning other things pertaining to her husband's fate. One night he let it slip that there will be a day when he does not come home in the evening. Another night she learns that his division will not leave until they are at "war strength," twenty percent above their peacetime capacity. The phrase haunts her: "As long as she lived she would never forget that phrase. She had never heard anything like it for condensing the hurt of war into a few innocent words; that twenty percent was to be the torn dead, the swathed passengers of the hospital trains—."[2] Today, as she watches the troops march in review on the parade ground to the music of a marching band, she looks at the general and reflects: "The General would come back, he would come back home some day. A lieutenant's chances were—well, they weren't quite so good—."[3] She wonders if the troops were marching slower than usual. Her throat tightens as she comes to the realization that the troops are not slow; rather, there are more of them:

> Now she understood. The whole division was "twenty percent over;" that was why it seemed to move past so slowly, why the last rank of his battalion was only now crossing her sight. . . . And she could feel a sickening tumble of something inside her, and her eyes seemed to flood with nothing at all, and she laid both hands on the rim of the chair-back.[4]

In Johnson's story a second woman, Mrs. Welles, has rented a series of rooms in army towns as she and her infant son follow her husband from assignment to assignment. The glamour magazines she reads are full of stories about women in the same straits:

> Here was Jinny, wife of Lieutenant Barry, having a baby and receiving a wire that lieutenant Barry was missing in action, and then receiving a wire that Lieutenant Barry was found, and in the next page Nannette, wife of Lieutenant Jim, also having a baby, receives a wire that Jim is missing, and he is, but the baby looks just like Jim. . . . Always the stuff of life, the pattern of life (no ladies' writer dared to be untimely), but so deodorized, so carefully culled from the Officers' Club, so scrubbed with Ivory and sprayed upon by cologne, so surrounded by chins lifted bravely in air, that the living reader felt ashamed of his mortality, abased with the knowledge of his doubt and cynicism and his chins tucked under chins—not proudly borne.[5]

She lives for the weekends when she can see her husband. At one point he does not come home. Some days later she received the inevitable phone call: "It came as she had expected it to come—when she stopped expecting it. 'You go back home,' Paul said. 'I'll let you know where they send me.'"[6] And so she goes through the familiar process of moving:

> In those last days after Paul had left, she felt strangely detached and unreal, as though in a foreign city and unable to speak an alien tongue. She went through the ritual of departure as in a mechanical dream. She called the few friends there had been time to make, and said good-bye. . . . She made reservations on the train, said good-bye . . . and packed herself slowly into a narrowing circle of the necessary things to be worn, to be eaten, to be slept in, in the final hours.[7]

Both women face the uncertainty war has brought to their lives. Both women feel very much alone. This theme of loneliness and isolation recurs in several stories.

Ruth Portugal's "Neither Here nor There" (1944; *Harper's Bazaar*, September, 1943) offers a darker perspective on the country's mobilization for war. In this story, a young woman, Caroline, is riding across the country on a train and encounters a soldier. She looks at him and, projecting the empathy she feels for her younger brother who has recently enlisted, feels "a helpless pity for the bewilderment and shock there must be behind that deliberately hardened face."[8] She observes the man for a day and then, by chance, is seated next to him in the club car, where he buys her a drink. She had been viewing the soldier from afar and has projected nobility to his service. Rather than a new recruit, however, it turns out that the soldier, Joe Purvis, has already served seven years, mostly overseas. As she converses with him his vocabulary becomes increasingly vulgar and it is apparent that he is far from noble. He concedes that he probably has "a couple of kids I don't know about."[9] She soon tries to disentangle her connection with the man, thinking "I would never have noticed him anywhere . . . were it not for the uniform . . . ."[10]

The next day she encounters him again. Purvis has won the pay of several recruits who had gambled with him the night before. He is utterly remorseless about taking advantage of the new recruits. Indeed, he holds them and people in general in disdain. Caroline is even more appalled: "She felt all the helpless rage and despair of the brother who might be signed over to the Joe Purvis sitting next to her . . . , who had never read a sonnet nor traced the design of a fugue . . . ."[11] She thinks about the prospect of an army of Purvises:

> Joe Purvis knew the craft of war. The war had proclaimed his existence . . . .
> Here in the direct, ignorant sureness of Joe Purvis of America was the brutality of the enemy. Facing her was his coarse primary maleness that somehow degraded her as it looked at her.[12]

Joe follows her to her sleeping compartment later and makes a crude advance toward her. When she rebuffs him, he attacks her verbally and physically: "You think I ain't fancy enough. Maybe I'm a bum, huh? The whole goddam country thinks I'm plenty good these days. I can take any goddam thing I want."[13] He holds her by the throat with one hand and then releases her. He walks away and, as he does, she thinks:

> She was rid of him, herself safe. And she was sad and cold in the wake of his shapeless loneliness. In that brief flash of loss he had shown at last a need. Even he did not want to be alone . . . . All the others like him, the mercenaries cut off from the world, were scattered now, nomads lost among the new millions of men bearing loyalties, who were usurping their garrisons.
>
> Someday there could be a leader—here, too, in America—who could take Joe Purvis and the ones like him and translate their inchoate power into a terrible thing. He would make them an army of occupation in their own land.[14]

Unlike the Giffords ("Boundary Line"), who are unaware of their own inclination toward fascism, Caroline sees clearly the delicate balance between a totalitarian society and a free society in wartime. The story appears as a tempering thought amidst the Donald Duck cartoons and other perky pro-war messages. Indeed, it was written as Japanese-Americans, many United States citizens, were being held prisoners in their own land.

Irwin Shaw is again prone to orating in "The Veterans Reflect" (1944; *Accent*, Winter, 1943). The story also bears striking parallels to two stories from the Great War. Just like the soldier in Jordan's "Vengeance is Mine" (1915), a soldier projects some two years in the future, at the end of the war. A returning veteran, Pete, is riding a train home and all around church bells are ringing, signaling the end of the war. In an adjacent seat a fat, loud businessman talks of his son, lost off Alaska two years before. Mostly, however, he talks about how the production of American business won the war. Peter reflects on his own losses: two cousins, a former roommate, and the men from his squadron. He thinks of all the graves, particularly the military cemetery adjacent to the hospital in which he had recovered from his wounds. He remembers joking with his nurse about the efficiency of the design. The nurse, who spends a great deal of her time weeping quietly behind a partition, does not get the joke. Peter reflects about his injuries and how, at the age of twenty-nine, he knew that he would always have to walk up and down stairs with care and that eating food would always be an adventure.

In yet another parallel, this time with Burt's "The Blood Red One," Peter thinks of the enemy leader, Hitler, at the close of the war. He imagines Hitler's thoughts as he rides through the mountains and hears church bells tolling the end of the war. Hitler, in Peter's mind, is bemoaning his fate, brooding over his army's defeat at the gates of Moscow.

Back in the American rail car, the businessman still boasts of American War production and Peter dreams of the forthcoming reunion with his wife and child. He wonders whether she'll think he has changed, or whether they will ever talk about the war. He resolves that he would tell her what it was like being shot in a falling plane with his mind focused on certain death. He would also tell her that it was worth it and that he would do it again.

Meanwhile, Hitler continues to brood from his car. How many times could his army have emerged victorious? The world certainly knew his name and millions has died because of him. They were so near to victory, but the idiots had let him down.

Back on the train car the loud voice of the businessman brays on, boasting that his son had died off the coast of Alaska and that business was producing 24 hours a day. Peter tries to slip back into his reverie, but the booming voice goes on and on, talking about business, communists, and his dead son." Peter can take no more. Peter tells the man to leave, and threatens to kill him. The offended businessman complies, but not without a final salvo, saying that he would have Peter arrested if it wasn't for his uniform. Peter closes his eyes and thinks of his waiting wife and child. Shaw, still with many clear misgivings about the war, concedes that it is necessary. There are nonetheless clear targets he addresses through the dialogue and disclosed thought.

Edward Fenton's "Burial in the Desert" (1945; *Harper's Bazaar*, October, 1944) takes us overseas for the first time, to a Middle Eastern desert and a casualty clearing station. Philip, an American ambulance driver, is typing a letter for a British soldier whose arms are immobilized in casts. The man has written to his mother and sister, assuring them that he is doing well. Philip asks: "Hadn't you better explain about the typing? . . . They might think there was something funny about it and worry."[15] They amend it: "A friend of mine is typing this letter for me, but it won't be long before I'll be writing you one myself."[16]

Philip is soon summoned by a soldier to help him and the chaplain with a task. They are to bury two dead soldiers. As they drive to the burial ground, Philip becomes queasy from "the sweet, sickening smell of decay had already begun to emanate from the dead passengers."[17] The soldier and chaplain are oblivious to the scent. As the Chaplain prepares for the service, Philip looks down at the "clumsily trussed bundles . . . . They looked so impossibly small! 'That's death,' Philip told himself. 'That's it.'"[18] The soldiers' identities are placed at the foot of their graves, sealed against the elements in pickle jars.

As the chaplain performs the service, Philip is distracted. He thinks back, months before, to a Mediterranean beach near Sid Barrani. He had tripped over a dead sea turtle, and as he continued to walk he passed over a ridge where he saw a "strange pile:"

> He could make out bits of clotted khaki cloth; a leg sticking up, its boot still on, but detached from what ever body it had once belonged to; a clenched, irrelevant hand; and formless, inert masses so caked into dust and blood that there

was no longer any conjecturing as to what they had been once . . . . The name-less reminders had been scooped up and assembled here for burial.[19]

He thought back to another scene on the road near El Alamein. He had come upon a wrecked Italian troop carrier, with dead, maggot infested driver still inside, being scavenged by a pair of British soldiers. He remembered his grandfather's funeral, but then brings himself back to the event at hand: "He stood there confronting death as a matter of accepted fact, part of his day's duty."[20] As they leave the cemetery, the ambulance kicks up a cloud of dust which "settles finally on the young olive trees and the fresh mounds, and on the pickle bottles, each of which held sealed against time and the Tunisian sky, a name, a rank, and a number."[21] The story emphasizes the cold brutality of war.

Meanwhile, the problems at home are not just about soldiers departing. Returning soldiers run into problems, too. Bill Gerry's "Understand What I Mean" (1945; *Yale Review*, Autumn, 1944) addresses the issue of race. A naval veteran goes back to his hometown and goes into to his old barber shop for a haircut. He waits his turn as the barber attends to an army sergeant. When the barber turns the chair around to face the window, a troop carrier rumbles by, bearing black soldiers. The sergeant comments: "More damn niggers!" The barber replies that more and more black soldiers have been shipped in, while still other blacks are working in local defense plants. He asks the sergeant where he is from and learns that the man is from Arkansas. The sergeant goes on: "An' I sure don' think mucha the way they run things out here either—lettin' niggers sit right next whites in the buses."[22] The sergeant continues to pontificate on his view of race and the barber cautions him that things are different in that part of the country.

The narrator tries to tune out the objectionable talk and thinks back to the time when his fellow postman, Brownie, whose route included this barber shop, had been inducted into the army. Brownie had been in an integrated unit and had found that the men could all work together: "It was swell. We ate together, slept in the same barracks, had a drill, and played ball a little. Just like I've always said it could be—understand what I mean?"[23]

The sergeant is getting ready to leave and pontificates once more: "'Guess I wouldn't get along out here,' he said. . . . Guess it's how you were brought up—what you're used to."[24] The narrator, who has now stepped up to the chair, replies: "You've got something there . . . . it's what you've been used to, all right. I'm from Massachusetts myself. "[25] He goes on to talk about how, when training in Texas, "I never got used to the old colored women with bundles or babies who always stood aside in pouring rains until every last man, young or old, climbed first into a bus."[26] At this point, who should walk in the door but Brownie, back in postal uniform.

Brownie sees the narrator, his friend, and immediately cracks a joke about the beauty parlor being across the street. The sergeant immediately takes offense and Brownie, sensing the tension, asks what is wrong. The narrator replies that they were "just trading viewpoints." He tells the sergeant that Brownie had also been a sergeant until a disagreement about a segregated bus that had ended with local policemen shooting him "full of holes."[27]

The sergeant responds: "So what're you squawkin' for? Ya had it comin', didn't ya?" Brownie replies: "I had it coming for ever believing that that uniform in wartime made one man as good as the next. I should have known better than to try to act decent."[28] Brownie stares at the sergeant and continues: "I was proud of that uniform . . . . I wanted to make good in it . . . . I was an officer's candidate."[29]

The sergeant retorts: "Thanks for the sob story, nigger. Next time you're down our way maybe you'll know better." The door bangs behind him. The narrator blocks Brownie from jumping out after him. He consoles his friend and those around him: "You should feel sorry for that poor guy . . . . He's young, the world's changing fast—and he's still got to grow up in it."[30] Brownies calms down and leaves. The narrator says aloud: "There goes a man—and a friend" (81). The barber resumes his clipping and, after a short silence, puts his own spin on the situation, commenting, without irony: "'Yeah—pretty good nigger, that one,' the old man said with indulgence."[31] The world was changing fast in other ways, too. With so many men away, at war, the dating scene has changed markedly.

Robert McLaughlin's "Poor Everybody" (1945; *New Yorker*, August 26, 1944) follows Lt. Bill Treanor on a leave to New York, where he is visiting the sister of his fiancée, Mary. Elly was fifteen when he last saw her, three years ago. Elly is now a mature, self-assured eighteen-year-old, with an uncomfortable resemblance to her older sister. Bill spends a night on the town with Elly that thrusts him uncomfortably into the fluid mores of wartime romance.

Elly's roommate, Marnie, separated from her Navy husband, is entertaining an Army corporal, who seems quite familiar with the apartment. Elly and Bill go to a club where they join a group of officers and dates: "Treanor never got the women straight, whether they were wives or pickups."[32] On the crowded cab ride across town to another club, Elly sits on Bill's lap, and teases that she should be marrying him. At the next club, an older gentleman, James, comes over to them and kisses Elly on the nape of her neck. James and Elly step aside and engage in a time of private conversation. When they return Bill asks Elly about him:

"Are you in love with him?"
"I guess so."
"You ought to be going with someone your own age."
Elly laughed. "That's a good one. Don't you know where to the good ones my age are?"[33]

Bill brusquely says it is time to take him home. Elly says that Marnie and her friend will be there. She suggests that they go to Bill's room. Bill refuses and drops her off at her apartment. They part, nonetheless, with a "hard kiss." As Bill leaves, Elly says gently: "'Poor Bill.' Then she added, 'And poor me. Poor

Mary. Poor everybody.'" Bill walks away and thinks: "He wanted a drink, and he wanted a woman. But mostly he wanted to be out of New York, out of America."[34]

Overseas, in England, the scene is no different. Lt. Lawrence Critchell's "Flesh and Blood" (1946; *Atlantic*, January, 1945) involves an army officer, Lt. Slack, and his struggles with loneliness. It is a Saturday night and Slack is moping around his base, near a small English town. Slack is desperately lonely and is doing all he can to avoid temptations of the flesh. He has stayed home from a Red Cross dance and thinks about being married and far away from home. War, he thinks, is easier on single men. It is hard to cope with the pressure of war and temptation when home was so far away.

After fretting for a while he catches a ride into town, to see a movie. He has seen the movie, however, and ends up walking around town. He thinks that maybe he should go to the dance. He figures that his wife would want him to go to the dance. His wife, he knew, trusted him, but he was not at all sure that he trusted himself. He thinks of his principles, but wonders about the relevance of his principles right now when teenagers were being killed all around him.

He hops to two or three bars and ends up in the line to see *Lifeboat*, the movie he'd already seen. An attractive, intelligent looking, English woman falls in line behind him. He buys her ticket. After the show, they walk around town, talking. She is separated from her husband and is saving up money for a divorce. Her husband, she thinks, is living with another woman. She asks about his wife. He speaks fondly and openly about her. The two eventually walk to the woman's home, where they sit on a log outside, smoking. She asks Slack if what they are doing seems wrong. He says no. She agrees, but adds that she thinks it should be, but sometimes you try to do the right thing and things just go wrong. They decide that they think too much.

Afterwards he walks home, thinking that it was hatred of the war that drove people to love. Slack returns to his base feeling more peaceful than he had felt in some time. He had put the events of the night away in his mind with all the other things about the war that he could never explain to the people back home.

Ruth Portugal provides a poignant glimpse of yet another domestic scene in "Call a Solemn Assembly" (1945; *Harper's Bazaar*, August, 1944) The setting is the June ceremony for boys graduating from Henry Hudson High School, Bronx, New York, in 1944. This year's class, at 400, is fifty per cent smaller than the usual class. Nearly half of the potential graduates have already joined the work force "making twenty-two fifty a week."[35] In the commencement program the names of eleven other potential graduates are marked by asterisks indicating that they are now in military service. Joan, the older sister of one of the graduates, Danny, reads the names of the eleven "with the asterisks catching at her like brambles." Her mother is likewise scanning the same list. Ruth thinks to herself:

"Danny won't be seventeen until August," was the quick prayer-like fact her mother would use as a shield against her alarm; before he would be eighteen

there was a year and two months. A year and two months—the war could be
over. If others—not Danny who had a year and two months—hurried, the war
might be over . . . . [36]

On either side of the speaking platform are service flags, one bearing the dates
1917-19 and the other, 1941-. The new flag already bears 33 gold stars. Joan
thinks about the dates one learns in school: Missouri Compromise, Civil War,
Panic of 1873. She thinks about time in a different way now: "But time was a
year and two months, it was until September, it was the day after tomorrow;
yesterday for the eleven with the asterisks beside their names. Time was one
clear harsh fact for the boys who were almost men in the June of 1944."[37]

The ceremony opens with the young men singing the National Anthem, a
song now omnipresent with the movies theatres playing it as "an overture
shipped from Hollywood, played at 3:30, 6:15, 9:00, and before the midnight
show on Saturday; the people standing, with an eye for a better seat, and mum-
bling through the one stanza and applauding and the show that they had paid to
see going on the screen at once."[38] Now, however, everyone stood in silence as
the boys sang through all the stanzas. Joan muses that this class was just learning to read when the Nazis burned books. By the time they started high school
France had been occupied. She thinks of how she had been such a supporter of
the war, the "Fight for Freedom." Now the war is far too personal for her: "I
have been arguing the fight for a long time and he will be the one to do the fighting, and she stood without moving beside her mother, locking the realization
inside herself. She was sick of talk."[39]

Special awards were presented to some students: "The First Prize in English
had been awarded, and as the boy was leaving the platform, the head said,
'Roger has been accepted as an Air Cadet.' For just the briefest fraction in time
the head's voice became a woman's troubled; proud of her prize pupil—and yet
troubled. A trace of a woman's anguish was in it, witnessing a woman's son
consigned to war."[40] The class has donated to the school a bronze plaque with
names of the thirty-three dead to be placed in the main corridor. The principal
rumbles on in an acceptance speech, dwelling on the thirty-three. Graduates
were then announced as each boy crossed the stage in a single line. Portugal
portrays the scene in periodic style:

> And so passed across the stage the boys who might have become scholars to
> help the world out of its long sickness; poets unrealized; the painters who might
> never paint . . .; the architects with the blueprints denied . . . ; the jive trumpet-
> ers who would never know . . . ; the four hundred private dreams that would
> have to be put away with other childish things. [41]

Joan watches as each boy passes in review, mindful that overseas sixteen-year-
olds were killing and being killed. She muses a silent plea:

*They cannot have been less loved than you, my brother. One they had sisters and mothers who tried to keep the world from bending them, who encouraged their dreams, and loved them very much, and feared for them. I am older than you and I cannot guide you anywhere from here. The years of our time are years of protest and that is the only thing I can promise you—my brother whom I have watched grow.[42]*

Across town, in Greenwich Village, Bessie Breuer's "Bury Your Own Dead" (1946; *Harper's Bazaar*, 1945) depicts a wrenching encounter between a WAC, Louisa, and an ex serviceman in a café. Both have emotional wounds from the war. They cope in different ways. The man, who looks as if he has done a good deal of drinking, invites himself to her table. The man admits that he is probably annoying her and says he will leave soon. He doesn't. The first thing he says is that she needs to straighten up her uniform (she had loosened her tie). Then he produces his military service record to show that he had been a major in the air corps. She knows now that she is in for the whole treatment. She observes to herself that one never saw the wounded and rejected in the recruiting offices and the training camps. Death was easily ignored. Now, however, she had to listen to the man while at the same time not letting a word he would say touch her. She thought about the pilots she had known—her pilot, Rab. He had left her without a goodbye. He had called her from Miami and that was it, except for the letters.

Her attention returns to the man at her table and she forces herself to ask him what is wrong. His younger brother, a paratrooper, is missing in France. He asks her if she has ever seen men die. She responds negatively, thinking that the dying was not part of her job. He has seen death, he says, and now his brother is dead. She thinks back to the news of Rab's death and the voice of his mother on the telephone from Nebraska and her personal grief. The man wants to go home with her. She refuses. He follows her to her apartment and she flees from him into the building. She bathes and prepares her clothes for the next day, thinking resolutely that she would not allow herself to get emotionally involved. The man would have to learn how to put it all away and live again as everyone else had.

Loneliness was not always self-imposed. Social, racial and ethnic groups were isolated from society, both voluntarily and involuntarily. Social distinction was the source of isolation in Edward Harris Heth's "Under the Ginkgo Tree" (1947; *Town and Country*, February, 1946). The story recounts the travails of two men lost in the jungle while trying to deliver a shipment of toilet paper to a base camp. The interesting dynamic here is the isolation of one of the soldiers, Lenicheck, who has been surrounded by a group of worldly Ivy Leaguers. He has passed for a Dartmouth man in his unit, but, while on his mission with Gill, a newcomer, he reveals that he is actually a high school dropout from Boise. Gill then manages to keep Lenicheck from panicking as they become lost in the jungle by regaling him with tales of the night life in New York city. It is the only story from World War II to address distinctions of social class in the military.

Of course the military was also a great unifier of diverse people. Irwin Shaw's "Gunners' Passage" (1945; *New Yorker*, July 22, 1944) depicts a day in the lives of three airmen as they await planes for passage to their new assignments. Stais, a Greek-American, war weary, nineteen year-old, sergeant, is being shipped home to Minnesota. Whitejack, a gunner and aerial photographer from North Carolina, and Novak, an Oklahoma farm boy turned radioman, are en route to India. Each man has seen a lot of combat. Whitehead is quite talkative, and tells the group of a leave in Rio where his crew had been lucky enough to encounter three American women from the embassy. Stais, dozing in and out of sleep, dreams of his various war experiences, lost for 14 days in Greece intermingled with thoughts of home. For a while he is interviewed by Novak, who is writing about Stais and his departure in a letter to his girlfriend in Long Island. She is not truly his girlfriend, Whitejack reminds him, as she is now going out with a tech sergeant. Novak continues to write her in spite of his change in status and the year and a half since he had seen her. The conversation is full of the intimate, almost incestuous, details commonly known by men who have lived and worked, desperately, in close quarters for an extended period of time. When Whitejack, tired of the chatter, leaves for a while, Novak tells Stais that Whitehead seemed changed, particularly after some friends had gone down. Stais thinks of how they had all changed. Stais dreams some more, now mixing his own memories with those of Novak and Whitejack.

Stais finally gets a plane and Whitejack walks over to the plane with him. Shaw writes of the contrast between the two men's futures. Stais was bound for home and family while Whitejack would return to the cold skies and more combat. Behind them they had shared so much together.

Another diverse bomber crew is profiled in A. J. Liebling's[43] "Run, Run, Run, Run" (*New Yorker*, September 29, 1945) In this story, a magazine reporter is attached to an American bomber squadron in Essex, England. It is late in the war, and the reporter, Meecham, has gone abroad as a replacement for another reporter, who has come home on leave. Meecham was a drama critic in the states, but all of his magazine colleagues had covered the war at one point or another and he feels left out. We join his experience as he ponders the guilt he feels in having withdrawn from a mission which he was scheduled to cover. Weather had been bad and the crew assured him that it would not clear. Meecham goes to London for a date. The weather eventually clears and the crew, whom Meecham had come to know quite well, had all died on their forty-first mission.

Meecham, an "untrammelled liberal," had been surprised that one much decorated member of the crew, Brownlea, was a leftist. Brownlea asked Meecham what he thinks of the Russians. Meecham, who "had heard talk at home about the Fascist mind of the Air Corps," had answered in a noncommittal fashion. Brownlea answers that he thinks the Russians are "the only hope I see for civilization."[44] The other crewmen do not care much about Russia either way, but Barry, from the West Coast, says he would rather be fighting the

Japanese: "I haven't got much against the Germans, except that Hitler is a son of a bitch." Elkan disagrees: "I'm a Jew, and they've been killing millions of Jews who didn't do a goddam thing to them. I hate the bastards and I like to think of what the bombs will do to them when we make our run."[45]

Meecham feels he must go on a mission now, and he hooks up with another plane, "Roll Me Over," some days later. This time he does not become attached to the crew. As they ride toward the mission, Meecham perceives that the motors seem to be saying "no, no, no, no." They complete the mission and he thinks they now say "run, run, run, run." Meecham returns to London, exhilarated, barely thinking of the dead crew. When he orders a second helping of oysters at a restaurant and is refused because of war shortages, he feels resentful. Maybe he should tell the man where he had just been. He realizes, however, that the man might well have sons killed or fighting with the R.A.F. "The thought recalled Barry and Brownlea and Elkan for the first time that day. Meecham wondered why it had seemed essential, that because of them, he go on a mission after they were dead." He does not dwell on the issue for long, however. He hopes his girlfriend is in town—"this ought to impress her."[46]

Francis L. Broderick's "Return by Faith" (1947; *Atlantic*, September, 1946) involves a veteran airman who has written to the family, the McShanes, of a colleague to tell them of the particulars of their son's death. Frank McShane has been reported as missing in action by army officials, even though other crews in his squadron had observed his plane burn and crash into the ocean. The McShanes have clung to every bit of doubt they can find in the government's letters to keep hoping for their son's return. The narrator, also named Frank, is trying to provide closure by telling them that their son did not survive.

After a face to face conversation with the family Mr. McShane responds: "Of course, we knew really in our hearts after your letter there was little reason for hope, but we hope anyway, especially Mrs. McShane. Somehow we'd feel disloyal to Frank to give up if there's any chance." [47] The family has taken a great deal of hope from a number of small things in which they see great significance. Emily, the baby of the family, who has never known her older brother, repeatedly tells her parents that "Frankie comin' home."[48] None of the government letters, they point out, say Frank is dead. Their priest, Father Ronald, told them to pray for Frank: ". . . I could tell from the look in his eyes he thought Frank would be back," Mrs. McShane says. Mrs. McShane showed one of the letters to the Mother Superior of the children's school: "she turned toward me with a gentle smile and said one day when Frank came home, he and his friend, Lieutenant Ryan, would laugh long over the gloom in that letter."[49]

As he leaves, narrator Frank is amazed by Mrs. McShane's faith:

She denied the reality of my eye witness account and accepted her hopes as undeniable truth. I saw again the flame over Togo Jima, the consuming heat which melted the wings . . . off its fuselage, the 14,000 foot plunge into the Pacific, the rescue planes searching eight hours for ten of the eleven men on the crew. . . . I did not need to remind myself that I saw those things happen, that Frank's death was a fact.[50]

He had brought the McShanes no comfort. Mrs. McShane hugged him as he left and said: "Oh, Frank! Do come back soon! I knew she was not talking to me."[51] In a notable reversal from the previous stories, this story is the only one from the second war to address issues of spiritual faith. The portrayal is quite skeptical.

Irwin Shaw, in his fourth and final war story, "Act of Faith" (1947; *New Yorker*, February 2, 1946) resolves the dilemma of anti-Semitism with a kind of civic faith. The story is yet another polemical, oratorical piece. A group of soldiers are trying to scrape together enough cash for a weekend in Paris (payroll has not caught up with them for three months). They sit around hatching plans for producing the money. One of the men, Seeger, has a German Luger, liberated from an SS major. His buddies point out that they could make nice money if he sold it.

We are now introduced to Seeger, who has just received a disturbing letter from his father. Seeger's brother, Jacob, who has already been discharged, his father reveals, was discharged on mental grounds. His father, has withheld the information until the war has ended, so as not to worry his son, and now recounts Jacob's erratic behavior. Jacob has developed a neurosis about being persecuted as a Jew. Every weapon, every political development has come to be a part of his oppression. The reaction, his father goes on to say, may not be all that abnormal. He, himself, finds people making remarks about Jews all around him. His father has reacted with a sense of self-loathing, avoiding any comment that might identify him as a stereotypical Jew. His father concedes that he had been scanning the lists of war dead in the paper, hoping to find Jewish names to prove that his kind were a part of the effort. The revelation of the atrocities suffered by Jews around the world has made Mr. Seeger wonder if all the Jews in the world disappeared that they might do themselves a service. The letter causes young Seeger to reflect, for the first time, on his own Jewishness.

He had been oblivious to the suffering of Jews when stateside, but had found a kinship to them in Europe. In each town they had liberated from the Germans people had stopped him, asking if he were a Jew. He never understood it until an old couple in Strabourg had asked him the question. The presence of a Jewish American soldier had been comforting to them. He began to realize what his presence meant to the people. Bitterly, he thinks it was silly of him to have pretended that he was like any other soldier in the war, after he had killed an S.S. major and taken the Luger from his dead body. He wondered if he should take the Luger home, loaded. He recalled the anti-Semitism he had heard in training camp and even during the war. He wonders, briefly, if it would have been better if he had died in battle. He quickly pulls himself out of such dark thoughts.

His buddies bring him back to the present and the issue at hand. He thinks of the tough times he has endured with his mates and how their lives had depended on each other. Seeger knows he will have to rely on these men at home just as he had in Europe. Seeger says he'll sell the Luger. His buddies want him to be sure. Seeger declares that he is sure, asking rhetorically whether he would have any use for it back home. Shaw ends his final war story with a surprisingly hopeful note, especially when compared with "Preach on the Dusty Roads."

Continuing the theme of anti-Semitism, J. D. Salinger's "A Girl I Knew" (1949; *Good Housekeeping*, February, 1948) is a chilling reminiscence about a Jewish, Austrian girl, Leah, that the narrator had known in Vienna before the war. He recalls their friendship with snippets of their conversations in broken English and German. When he returned to the states, he thought of Leah each time he heard of the German invasion of Austria. Later, when the United States entered the war, he served in the Army and, shortly after the war's end, was sent to Austria. He went to the old neighborhood and, after inquiring, was told that Leah was dead. He goes to his old apartment building, now converted to officers' quarters for American soldiers. He asks if he can go up to where her family's apartment once was. The bored staff sergeant in charge does not want to let him in. The two men then engage in a rather pointed conversation about the reasons for visiting the apartment. When told that the young woman and her family were executed the sergeant asks if she was a Jew.

The sergeant finally allows him to enter the apartment. Everything about it has changed. He stands on the balcony for a while, thanks the sergeant and leaves.

Race and ethnicity are also a factor in Beatrice Griffith's "In the Flow of Time" (1949; *Common Ground*, 1948). The story is set in Los Angeles, in 1943, during the "Zootsuit Riots." The narrator, Danny, and his friend, Mingo, have taken the streetcar out to his grandfather's farm (Danny's family has lived in California since gold rush days) in the San Fernando Valley the day before they are to be inducted into the army. They are wearing their zootsuits for a party at Danny's house later that evening.

Coming back into Los Angeles, on the street car, people stare at their clothing. They leave the street car at Hill Street, where soldiers, sailors, and marines are roaming about brandishing bottles, iron bars, belts, and clubs. A crowd gathered there screams encouragement as Pachucos are chased down, beaten, and stripped of the offending clothing. Police stand by, doing nothing. Danny and Mingo avoid the scene by passing through an alley way. The next street, however, is the scene of even more intense action as a street car is stopped by a group of sailors and marines. One of the men screams out that they are going to get the zootsuits. Mingo becomes incredulously furious, remarking that the scene they are witnessing looks like it is taking place in Germany.

The two boys finally catch a street car to Danny's house. His sister, Dora, reports that her boyfriend has been beaten and his clothes stripped off his back. Suddenly, a group of drunken sailors and marines comes into Danny's home, bashing it and its inhabitants. Danny's mother screams at them, telling the men that they are disgracing their uniforms. After the assault has ended, Danny and Mingo sit, bruised and bloodied, on the back step. Mingo, still raging, vows to go to Mexico and join the Mexican forces. When Danny tries to say that the army is different, Mingo doesn't buy it. Danny tries hard to talk Mingo out of his rage. He tells him about how his brother brought two of his white buddies home with him on leave. The men stayed in their home and ate at their table. Now they fly together as a bomber crew in Germany. They treat each other like brothers. Mingo retorts that you shouldn't have to wear a uniform to be treated like a brother.

Mingo leaves Danny with their argument unresolved. Danny sits on the steps, thinking that in the future we will have to raise our children in a way that will prevent things like the riots from happening. As he sits, articulating his silent prayer of hope, he still hears the sirens blaring downtown.

The failure of American race relations is further displayed in a story about the residual casualties of war. Kay Boyle's "The Lost" (1952: *Tomorrow*, March, 1951) is a moving story about war orphans in Europe. Many orphans attached themselves to military units, whose well intentioned soldiers promised the boys they could go home with them after the war (One such orphan was featured in the long-running comic strip, "Dondi."). In Boyle's story three boys, are delivered to an administrative center for processing. The three boys, aged 12-15, are dressed in cut down G.I. clothing, and, even though they are Czech, Italian, and Polish by birth, they speak American English, one with a Southern and another with a Brooklyn accent. Soldiers have promised they would sneak them aboard troop transports at Bremerhaven. M.P.s interfered with their plans. One of the boys, Janos, who saw his parents hanged in Noverzcimki, had been befriended by a man from Chattanooga, Charlie Madden, who promised to adopt him after the war. There is an unfortunate catch, though. Charlie Madden is black. The social worker has the unfortunate task of explaining to Janos why he could never go to the United States with Madden. Boyle describes how the clerk, in explaining the stark facts, transformed from being a woman, or even a human being, into a faltering, disembodied voice saying no. Janos, faced with the prospect of being adopted by a white American family, eventually runs away, leaving behind a note for Charlie Madden. The note, written in broken English, tells Charlie Madden that Janos has received good news. His family has been found and Janos will be returning to them. Again, the war points to dysfunction at home. Even our acts of charity must be filtered through the sieve of Jim Crow.

In war, people are displaced, both physically and in spirit. Martha Gellhorn's "Weekend at Grimsby" (1952; *Atlantic*, May, 1951) is about a former war correspondent, Lily Cameron, on her way to Grimsby, on the English coast, to visit her friends, Sim and Marek, former Polish Lancers relocated in England. Lily has been to Grimsby once before. On a Christmas during the war she visited friends with a bomber group stationed there. Three days later she had received word that her friend, John, had been killed in a flight over Berlin. As Lily muses to herself during the long, cold, train ride through rainy England, she thinks that she did not think about the dead during the war, but that she had been doing little else since. The dead still live with her.

During the war, Lily had traveled across Italy with Sim, Marek, and their regiment of Polish forces. Sim and Marek are now part owners of a pair of struggling fishing boats. The two seem barely able to eke out an existence. The three dine in on a meager, but elegantly served meal in Sim's small house. The scene depresses Lily, but Sim is a survivor. Lily looks at a youthful picture of him standing front of his family home, later occupied by Germans, Russians, and various others. Again, we see the contents of her mind. Sim, a Polish Prince lost six of ten family members during the war. Marek had lost his wife and two children.

Marek talks of returning to Poland to fight the Russians, but Lily responds that that she wants no more part of war. War, she says, produces no good. Nothing good comes of it. Marek replies that war isn't meant to serve a purpose, except to give men a little excitement between living and dying.

Lily's friends enjoy hosting her, but Lilly cannot snap out of her depression. Later in the evening, after Marek had gone to his home, Sim makes a pass at Lily, with whom he had been intimate during the war. Lily refuses politely, and, in the conversation afterwards, Sim realizes that Lily is still in love with a dead fighter pilot. Everything now makes sense to Sim. He tells Lilly that a person cannot live if they are still in love with the dead.

The next day, Marek and Sim introduce Lily to their friend, Grace, a large, ungainly, young woman. Marek tells Lily that Sim and Grace are to be married. Lily's facial expression betrays her disgust at the idea. Marek tells Lilly that Grace loves Sim and, more importantly, Grace is not afraid of the life they will lead together. Marek concedes that maybe one has to be a Pole to understand. Although bad things happen, Poles know that one has to let the past go and live the life they have. He tells Lilly she can never live again if she clings to the past. As Lily returns to London on the train, later that evening, she thinks about her life. She wonders how she could learn to live after having gone so long in the opposite direction.

Harris Downey takes yet another view of courage and survival in two stories published in the early fifties. The first, "The Hunters" (1951; *Epoch*, Summer, 1950), is a tale about a young man trying to survive in the shock, chaos, and moral ambiguity of war. The second examines another type of courage, embodied in the actions of two average soldiers.

In "The Hunters," a young soldier, Private Meadows, has become separated from his unit, somewhere in the North of France. His life had been "torpor" ever since his arrival in France. Since his arrival in France, time, direction, indeed reality, had all become meaningless to him: "He had seen his enemy and his comrades sprawled grotesque and cold in the neutrality of death, as impersonal as the cows among them, angling stiff legs into the sky."[52] He had thrown grenades, shot at anonymous men, and seen the destruction of French villages. His surroundings were unreal: "He had seen a dog tethered at the gate, howl at the noise of destruction and die in terror; he had seen bees swarm from their hives at the ground shake of cannon and hang in the air, directionless."[53] None of this had touched him, however: "He had left himself some where, and the farther he walked the terrain of war, the farther he went from himself."[54] Survival had simply been a matter of following his comrades from one place to the next.

Now, having lost sight of his colleagues in a wooded area, he frantically tries to find them. Eventually, he meets another man, also detached, but from a different unit. The other soldier, a "big man," leads Meadows on until they encounter a German soldier, whom they discover, upon capturing and searching, is carrying a payroll. The other soldier orders Meadows to take the money, commands the German to "Vamoos," and then calmly shoots the man in the back. The big man divvies up the money and thrusts half of it to Meadows. Sometime later they hear the sound of artillery and planes. One plane it hit and its crew parachutes toward them. The big man proceeds to shoot one of the parachutists and commands Meadows to shoot another. Meadows mindlessly obeys, though balks at shooting another.

Eventually the men reach a village and find their units. Restored to the companionship of his company, Meadows sits and, still clutching the German money, begins to weep "convulsively." His refound buddies tell him to "snap out of it." After all, it is "time for chow."[55]

"Crispin's Way" (1953; *Epoch*, Fall, 1952) features another confused young soldier, Corporal Crispin, interred in a German Prisoner of War camp. Crispin has been in the camp for eleven weeks, but recently transferred to a special camp. The Germans have been trying to break him, to get him to perform duties of which he is not quite aware. They tell him: "You are American. You are handsome. You are serious. You are sincere."[56] His only regular contact is with an Englishman named Riddle and an American named Chance. He distrusts Riddle, but is drawn to Chance: "Chance was American. He was affable, talkative, cheerful." He shows Crispin the ropes of the camp. "At night he came into Crispin's room, slipped off his shoes, sat across the narrow bunk with his feet drawn up under him and his back against the wall and talked of home." [57] Crispin was still a little wary of Chance, and wondered what his duties were in the special camp.

Later, the Englishman, Riddle, approaches him in his room. Riddle asks if Crispin has figured out why the German's want him. Crispin says no and Riddle tells him: "Your hair. Your curly yellow hair. ... And your American ways."[58] Riddle leaves and Crispin goes on with his mysterious existence. The next day the Germans tell Crispin they could use him against the Bolsheviks. Crispin refuses to cooperate. On the following day, however, he is seduced by a pretty German kitchen maid and caught by the Germans. Now, he has committed a crime by seducing a "native woman." The "crime" serves to strip him of his prisoner of war status. He must cooperate or die.

Sergeant Chance meets him back at his room, "hand outstretched in welcome, teeth gleaming."[59] Chance, it turns out, is one of them. He had gone over to the Germans. His job is to orient Crispin for his job. Chance tells Crispin that he'll be sent out "to live with other prisoners. The new ones. And get informa-

tion from them. See, you're the sort. Fellows will trust you."[60] Chance continues
to chat with Crispin:

> Crispin lay on the bunk, waiting for the sergeant to finish his story and leave.
> Now he was competent of choice, of a lasting valid choice. It seemed all the
> while the competence had been in him, hidden in the darkness of his jumbled
> thoughts, awaiting his recognition of it. His treacherous consent had never been
> real; only now did he see through its masquerade. He knew what he must do;
> handcuffs and blows and threats would be useless against his denial. And
> though he doubted whether they would kill him, he knew now that the doubt
> was not the root of his courage.[61]

Once Crispin was fully aware of his situation, his resolve was set. When consequences are clear, An American makes up his mind. This is the rare World War
II story (though published 7 years after the war's end) that seems to strike the
chords of patriotism. One can almost hear echoes of Nathan Hale's mythic line
in the background: "I regret that I have but one life to give for my country."
Downey's two stories, put together, portray both the strength and weaknesses of
the American fighting force. The soldiers, many of them quite young and imma-
ture, could be easily led and influenced to do horrible, but sometimes necessary,
things. Within them is also a strong moral compass that often manifests itself in
issues such as loyalty.

Edward Newhouse's "My Brother's Second Funeral" (1950; *New Yorker*,
1949) closes the accounts from the World War II era with a realist's look at war
and death that takes on a somewhat wry and cynical fashion, criticizing the way
we celebrate death and war, particularly in small towns. Bob, the narrator, tells
of the hoopla surrounding the reinterment of his brother, Riley, who was killed
at Anzio. Their father served in World War I in a non-combat role and has been
active in the American Legion ever since. The father has arranged for an elabo-
rate reburial of Riley, in his home town, with a great deal of fanfare. Bob, also a
combat veteran, reports that he and his brother were both somewhat embarrassed
by the Legionnaires antics on Memorial Day. He sums it up as follows:

> If, back in '17, they had stuck my father into some infantry line unit, it might
> have been another story. Instead, they went and made him a staff general's or-
> derly, and he spent almost a year in Paris. That's what he never got over. They
> gave him that dog robber's job, and it's still the big thing in his life. You'll find
> a few men like that in every Legion post, and usually they do most of the
> sounding off.[62]

Bob recalls that Riley used to have extensive arguments with their father: "Back
in the war, the old man said, the Germans used to kill Belgian babies. Riley said
all that's been proved to be nothing but propaganda."[63]

Riley's death hit their father hard. He sat around for a week, doing nothing.
Then, he turned Riley's old bedroom into a shrine. He got the Legion Post to
name itself after Riley. And now the funeral. At the planning session with their

Pastor, Bob takes exception to the presence of a group of Girl Scouts. The Pastor responds: "Those little girls wish to pay their last respects, Bob. . . . Riley gave his life that they might live in peace and plenty."[64] Bob responds with a speech that many a combat veteran would have liked to make:

> I knew Riley. I slept in the same bed with him for thirteen years. He didn't give his life, and neither did anybody else I knew overseas. People got killed. They had no choice about it. Sometimes it looked as if they did, but they didn't. Riley was hit by a piece of steel. And if he knew his bones were going to be dug up so they can be buried again, with a band playing and people popping guns in the air—.[65]

Bob's oration is cut off by his mother.

Later, Bob is asked by his mother to accompany her to the chapel, were she wants to pray. He walks her there, but won't pray: "'I don't know how to pray,' I said. 'Sometimes I'd like to, but I don't know how.'"[66] Bob does not attend the funeral. He can't say why his brother died. He knows the funeral will go off as planned. His father will be pleased with it all: "You can't blame a man for having spent his best year as a soldier in Paris. You can't blame old Mr. Haislip for repeating once more that my brother gave his life. But I don't want to be there to hear it."[67] Bob's tone is realistic. The idea of war as serving a higher purpose, so popular in the aftermath of the first war, is dismissed.

# Later Revisions

Some significant stories from the war remained untold for many years. Though the concentration camps are alluded to in stories written during the war years, particular details of the Holocaust were passed over lightly. In 1955 Alain Resnais' documentary, "Night and Fog," depicted the human tragedy on film with graphic archival footage, but it is not until 1982 that a story in the series provides an account. Ian MacMillan's "Proud Monster—Sketches" (*Carolina Quarterly*, 1981) is a series of eight vignettes, each datelined with a specific time and place, spanning the war, but not in any particular order.

The first vignette, set in Treblinka in mid war, depicts two men, Poles, assigned to the job of burying dead bodies from the concentration camp. The unclothed bodies arrive in a rail cart and are to be buried six levels deep in a trench. One of the men sees the body of a beautiful, plump, buxom girl. He touches the girl's breast only to find that he has forced air out of her mouth with his touch. The men talk about an officer who is said to shoot children for fun in the presence of his young daughter, who take pleasure in watching. The men agree it is not a thing for children to see. The next scene is set in Auschwitz, where a starving child is comforted by a science book he has carefully kept concealed. It speaks of the linear magnitude of time. Somehow the earth's ancientness makes him feel secure in his grim, but brief, moment of existence. In another scene, set in Berlin at the close of the war, a man cowers in his home as Russian troops approach. The troops discover him and his wife and daughter, both dead. The soldiers genuflect and pray. The soldiers then move on, leaving the man with his dead family.

A scene set in Poland, earlier in the war, describes a group of boys being forced to clean the stones of the town square with their tongues before being relocated to the Janowska Camp. In another vignette from 1945 we are given details of a ghastly nightmare. A mother and small daughter are walking wearily toward a refugee camp. The woman orders a meal at a nearby restaurant. She is served a plate of meat, which she grimly discovers is part of a child's upper arm. She awakes from her dream frantically clutching at her child to assure that she still has all of her limbs.

Back in 1941, in Poland, an SS administrator ransacks the house of a Polish leader, looking for his stamp collection. He finds the rare stamp he is seeking, as the man and a pregnant woman are executed outside. Only later does he discover that the stamp is a forgery. A scene from Russia in mid war describes three German soldiers retreating in the snow toward the Polish border. One man repeatedly tells stories of the SS executing women and children in Siedlice. The final scene, set in Poland in 1945, portrays a German sniper lying on a hillside, watching the locals greet the Russian troops, his rifle randomly killing targets in the village below. The story, realistic and grimly matter of fact, is reminiscent of March's "Fifteen from Company K."

A second significant issue is the internment of Japanese-Americans during the war. The first mention of internment does not come until 1971, twenty-six years after the end of World War II. Albert Drake's "The Chicken Which Became a Rat" (*Northwest Review*, Summer, 1970), a story, narrated by a young boy, is set in Oregon. He writes of how he and the other neighborhood children had fortified the area with foxholes and trenches after Pearl Harbor. And he writes of how he, the other children, and his Uncle Boswick, harassed a "Jap" who lived in a tarpaper shack adjacent to their property. It was late in the war, and the man, an American citizen, who had lost his farm near Gresham, had been released from an internment camp. Our narrator, fueled by the cover of *Liberty* portraying Tojo as a spider and a *Life* article that tells how to distinguish Japanese from Chinese, carries on relentless surveillance of his Japanese neighbor, who was earnestly trying to grow produce on a modest stretch of land.

One summer day the Japanese man startles the narrator, who was crawling through the garden, on his stomach, wearing a gas mask. He flees the scene, leaving his mask behind. A short time later the Japanese man appears at his mother's door with the gasmask filled with vegetables. The boy's mother says she will pay the man a quarter a week for fresh vegetables. He hopes to save the money to buy some chickens.

The following Autumn, 1944, one of the neighbors' fathers is killed in the war and the family moved to Seattle. Another neighbor sends a crate of souvenirs, Japanese swords and rifles, home. Spring arrived and the Japanese neighbor resumed working in his garden and building a chicken coop. VE-day arrives and the neighbor with the trunk of souvenirs arrives home. One day, as his wife is clearing brush with one of the swords, he cuts off her head with the sword and then kills himself with one of the rifles.

Meanwhile the Japanese neighbor is doing peculiar things with his chickens. He does not collect the eggs, will not sell them, and also seems to have stopped feeding the birds. When Uncle Boswick goes over to inquire about the eggs, he tells the incredulous man that he won't eat the eggs of the hens with whom he is personally familiar. The narrator, ever spying on the scene through his binoculars, observes one day a weird event. A baby chick pecks its way out of its shell, only to be eaten by its mother. Soon, the entire chicken coop is a scene of carnage, as the chickens proceed to devour the remaining eggs and, then, each other. By the end of five days, only one chicken remained. Soon thereafter, the war in Japan ends. The narrator goes over to the "Jap's" house, but finds that the man has packed up and left. The only remnant of human occupation was a collection of newspaper clippings, pasted to the wall that detailed the progress of the war. The most recent clipping was dated two days earlier. He looks in the chicken coop and notices movement from a burlap bag. Out from the bag emerged the surviving chicken, smelly and devoid of feathers. Her skin was black. The chick looked like a rat. The emergence of the mutated beast is described as a triumph.

Tom Robbins, "The Chink and the Clock People," (1977; *American Review*, 1976) is the only other story to refer to the issue of internment of Japanese-Americans during World War II. Though not about the war in particular, it does feature a character, known as "The Chink," who was marked by that experience. The Chink immigrated to the United States when he was 8 years old and became a naturalized citizen. After high school he worked as a gardener at Cal Berkeley, where, over the course of 12 years, he also took a number of college courses. When the war broke out the Chink was relocated to the internment camp at Tule Lake. As Robbins writes, loyal Japanese-Americans were segregated from disloyal ones. When asked if he supported the war effort, the chink had responded negatively. He was soon sent to the Tule Lake internment camp. The Chink asked to be sent to another camp, with his family. Unfortunately, his FBI check showed that his eclectic pursuit of life and happiness, including relations with white women, made him dangerous. His request was denied. When trouble broke out at the camp he was sent to the stockade. From there he escaped by digging a tunnel out of camp.

The Chink traveled through the mountain, working for times as a farm laborer. Not many farmers could distinguish Japanese from Hispanics. Eventually, he takes up with the "clock people," a group of native Americans from various tribes, who formed a culture in the mountains of Northern California. The clock people, whose diverse tribes had been misnamed "Indians," similarly misnamed their new Japanese-American friend, "Chink."

The stories of World War Two have taken us from the streets of New York to the jungles of South Asia and back again. We've met men and women, civilians and soldiers. Though the stories have certainly portrayed issues of war, they have also raised domestic issues that will be at the forefront of the American democracy well into the seventies. The intentionality of these stories is much more implicit than the stories of the Great War. Some characters still give speeches, particularly in Shaw's stories, but for the most part the rhetorical dimension is depicted in the scene presented. Characters might give speeches in their inner monologues, but more often the action of the story provides its rhetorical impetus. The stories do not feature outright opposition to the war. The climate of the times was not favorable to such expression. The stories do not, however, endorse the war either. Rather, the war is treated as an event which must be endured, like a bad dream. The signs of division in the stories are transmitted through the depiction, the verbal pictures that can say so much more than mere words. Most notable is the way in which the scenes depicted in the stories portray the cracks in the American tableau. Racism, anti-Semitism, classicism, and male chauvinism are clearly brought under scrutiny. In stark contrast to the Great War, women are given voice. In Burkean terms, the stories focus largely on act and scene. Absent is any mystical purpose or agent centered focus. The feeling seems to be one that a straight depiction of the facts would present the reader with inevitable conclusions. For the most part, the trend continues in the stories to follow. Nonetheless, the post-war stories tend to be a little more obvious in showing the writer's point of view.

# Notes

1. Berry Fleming, "Strike Up the Stirring Music," in Martha Foley, Martha, ed., *Best American Short Stories, 1944, and Yearbook of the American Short Story* (Boston: Houghton Mifflin, 1944) 118.
2. Fleming 126.
3. Fleming 120.
4. Fleming 124.
5. Josephine Johnson, "The Rented Room," in Martha Foley, ed., *Best American Short Stories, 1944, and Yearbook of the American Short Story* (Boston: Houghton Mifflin, 1944) 149.
6. Johnson 161.
7. Johnson 162.
8. Ruth Portugal, "Neither Here nor There," in Martha Foley, ed., *Best American Short Stories, 1944, and Yearbook of the American Short Story* (Boston: Houghton Mifflin, 1944) 295.
9. Portugal, "Neither," 299
10. Portugal, "Neither," 301.
11. Portugal, "Neither," 303.
12. Portugal, "Neither," 303.
13. Portugal, "Neither," 307.
14. Portugal, "Neither," 308.
15. Edward Fenton, "Burial in the Desert," in Martha Foley, Martha, ed., *Best American Short Stories, 1945, and Yearbook of the American Short Story* (Boston: Houghton Mifflin, 1945) 50.
16. Fenton 51.
17. Fenton 52.
18. Fenton 54.
19. Fenton 56.
20. Fenton 59.
21. Fenton 63.
22. Bill Gerry, "Understand What I Mean," in Martha Foley, ed., *Best American Short Stories, 1945, and Yearbook of the American Short Story* (Boston: Houghton Mifflin, 1945) 73.
23. Gerry 74-75.
24. Gerry 76.
25. Gerry 76.
26. Gerry 77.
27. Gerry 79.
28. Gerry 79.
29. Gerry 80.
30. Gerry 80.
31. Gerry 81.

32. Robert McLaughlin, "Poor Everybody," in Martha Foley, ed., *Best American Short Stories, 1945, and Yearbook of the American Short Story* (Boston: Houghton Mifflin, 1945) 129.

33. McLaughlin 131.

34. McLaughlin 132.

35. Ruth Portugal, "Call a Solemn Assembly," in Martha Foley, ed., *Best American Short Stories, 1945, and Yearbook of the American Short Story* (Boston: Houghton Mifflin, 1945) 170.

36. Portugal, "Call," 171. Ellipses in the original.

37. Portugal, "Call," 172.

38. Portugal, "Call," 174.

39. Portugal, "Call," 175.

40. Portugal, "Call," 176.

41. Portugal, "Call," 178.

42. Portugal, "Call," 179.

43. Liebling was a European correspondent for the *New Yorker.* At least one of his dispatches, later reprinted, featured a profile on a fighter squadron. See A. J. Liebling, "The Foamy Fields," *in Just Enough Liebling: Classic Work by the Legendary New Yorker Writer* (New York: North Point Press, 2004) pp. 105-48.

44. A. J. Liebling, A. J., "Run, Run, Run, Run, " in Martha Foley, ed., *Best American Short Stories, 1946, and Yearbook of the American Short Story* (Boston: Houghton Mifflin, 1946) 264.

45. Liebling 262.

46. Liebling 276.

47. Francis Broderick, "Return by Faith," in Martha Foley, ed., *Best American Short Stories, 1947, and Yearbook of the American Short Story* (Boston: Houghton Mifflin, 1947) 8-9.

48. Broderick 11.

49. Broderick 15.

50. Broderick 16.

51. Broderick 16.

52. Harris Downey, "The Hunters," in Martha Foley, ed., *Best American Short Stories, 1951, and Yearbook of the American Short Story* (Boston: Houghton Mifflin, 1951) 100.

53. Downey, "The Hunters," 100-01.

54. Downey, "The Hunters," 100.

55. Downey, The Hunters," 114.

56. Harris Downey, "Crispin's Way," in Martha Foley, ed., *Best American Short Stories, 1953, and Yearbook of the American Short Story* (Boston: Houghton Mifflin, 1953) 103.

57. Downey, "Crispin's Way," 105.

58. Downey, "Crispin's Way," 108.

59. Downey, "Crispin's Way," 109.

60. Downey, "Crispin's Way," 110.

61. Downey, "Crispin's Way," 110-11.

62. Edward Newhouse, "My Brother's Second Funeral," in Martha Foley, ed., *Best American Short Stories, 1950, and Yearbook of the American Short Story* (Boston: Houghton Mifflin, 1950) 318.

63. Newhouse 319.

64. Newhouse 323.

65. Newhouse 323-24.
66. Newhouse 326.
67. Newhouse 327.

# Chapter Four
# Beyond the War

Stories with some connection to World War II continue, sporadically, into the 1980s. But while the earlier stories address the war and its aftermath, the next group is rather self-absorbed in looking at the present. With military service almost universal for able bodied men between World War II and the early Vietnam era, the stories now begin to share a common roar of protest against the sadistic brutality of basic training and the routine "chickenshit" of military service in general. Nearly half of the stories after 1947 deal with basic training in some fashion. Integrally imbedded in the stories, however, is an acknowledgement of other things occurring in American society, particularly tensions concerning race and ethnicity. The stories become less implicit. The characters let us know what they think. Vietnam seems to appear in the volumes at a relatively late date, 1969, and, of course, the nature of those stories is radically unlike accounts of earlier wars.

Popular song remained relatively static in the early post-war years. Instrumentals began to give way to vocals, but the lyrics were not particularly a reflection of current events. The Broadway musical, "South Pacific," (1949) touched on issues on racism, particularly in the song "You've Got to Be Carefully Taught." Films, on the other hand, addressed a number of current issues. 1947 saw "The Best Years of Our Lives," a film about veterans attempting to readjust to civilian life and "Gentleman's Agreement," a film addressing discrimination against Jews. 1950 featured "Now Way Out," a tense film in which a hostile, racist convict, played by Richard Widmark, is treated by a black physician (Sidney Poitier) in a prison ward. Black white relations were again visited in 1958 in "The Defiant Ones." In this film Poitier is cast as prison escapee who is handcuffed to a white convict, played by Tony Curtis. By the mid fifties rock and roll began to become a mainstay of the popular music scene. Elvis Presley had hits in 1956 with "Hound Dog," "Don't Be Cruel," and "Heartbreak Hotel." Pat

Boone, Chuck Berry, and Buddy Holly joined Elvis with popular hits in 1957. And Elvis, who had become a move star, appearing in "Jailhouse Rock" (1957) and "King Creole" (1958), served a two-year hitch in the army.

The post war period still features stories written about the division and romance of the Civil War. John Bell Clayton's "Visitor from Philadelphia" (1948; *Harper's,* 1947) involves a young Virginia boy playing in his yard with another boy, Willard, whom we learn is visiting from Philadelphia. Upon being invited into the house, the visitor sees a picture of a man in a Confederate uniform hanging over the mantle. The boys talk about the picture. Willard, who can reference no wars other than those fought with Germans, opines that the uniform looks like one of a Western Union messenger. He asks:

> "What kind of bush-league war did he fight in?"
> Through the open window I heard Grandma clear her throat.
> "The War Between the States," I said.
> "Never heard of it," Willard said flatly. "World War.And the Revolutionary War and the Civil War."[1]

The boy's grandmother cleared her throat again. She tells Willard that the picture is of her brother, who was a general in the Confederate Army. Willard responded with a grin, saying, "How much does that make eggs sell for?"[2]
The grandmother responds with a tirade against General Grant and proclaims with pride that she never blamed her brother for burning Chambersburg, PA. Willard responds that Chambersburg was in his state. He tells the grandmother that she should be ashamed to have such a barbarian's picture hanging in her house. She tells Willard to leave. Willard departs, calling out that the boy and his grandmother are "cuckoos." This story highlights the fact that divisions from the Civil War are very much alive, even as advances in racial relations begin to be made. As we shall see a little later, the romance of the Civil War remains as well. Meanwhile, the stories address a variety of lingering problems.

George P. Elliott's "The NRACP" (1950; *Hudson Review,* 1949) presents a troubling reflection of the post-World War II climate and our nation's struggles with racial equality. Elliot echoes earlier writers in wondering how far America is from Nazi Germany. The National Relocation Authority: Colored Persons (NRACP) is an administrative agency formed to deal with the "Negro question." Our central protagonist, a public relations officer for the NRACP, discovers the answer and comments on it in a series of letters written to his friends from a relocation center somewhere in the west. He has come to realize, slowly, that Negroes are being relocated, slaughtered, and fed to the NRACP bureaucrats, including himself. In his abject horror he reflects on the factors that have brought him to this point. The American system of government by the people, he says, is the ultimate result of a leaderless country ruled by natural law:

> It is odd that we Americans have no leader; what we have is committees and boards and bureau heads who collectively possess leadership and direct our

way almost impersonally. There is nothing whatsoever that I myself would like so much as to be one of those wise, courageous, anonymous planners. The wisdom I think that I possess. But in place of courage I have a set of moral scruples dating from an era when man was supposed to have a soul and when disease took care of overpopulation. The old vestigial values of Christianity must be excised in the people as they are being excised in me. The good and the lucky are assisting at the birth of a new age. The weak and unfit are perishing in the death of an old. Which shall it be for us?"[3]

The author goes on to invoke an event well documented by Picasso: "Remember, back in the simple days of the Spanish Civil War, when Guernica was bombed, we speculated all one evening what the worst thing in the world could be? This is the worst thing in the world, Herb. I tell you, the worst. After this, nothing."[4] Fifty years later, however, in our time, the worst things continue. Elliott grapples with the eternal questions about individual responsibility when working within a system in an atmosphere of war.

# Psychiatric Wards

Three stories present yet another aspect of war and its aftermath, the mentally ill in the care of the military. In Irving Pfeffer's "All Prisoners Here," (1949; *Harper's*, 1948) the scene is a ward in a naval hospital. Pharmacist's Mate Norden has been awakened at his desk, where he stands night watch, with a new admit. As he gets the new man settled, we get a glimpse of the activity in the ward at night. One man, Garnes, had been shot through the back when he tried to escape detention. He lays uncomfortably in his bed as his wound drips audibly into a drain pan. Nearby, he hears hurried breathing, whimpers, and screams from Morrison, who is struggling with a bout of Malaria. Another man, Rosbrough, is delusional and goes to the latrine, where he sits on the floor in darkness. Norden brings Rosbrough back to his bunk, but Rosbrough eventually attacks Morrison, who is reliving an air raid in his delirium. While Norden and the night Officer, who has just arrived, struggle to pull Rosbrough off of Morrison, Kummer, the newly admitted man, sneaks into the latrine and hangs himself. Garnes sees it all happen, but cannot move because of his wound. When Norden returns to his desk he nods off again, only to dream of the night's misfortunes.

Leo Rosten's "The Guy in Ward 4" (1959; *Harper's*, 1958) portrays a few weeks in the life of an Army psychiatrist, Dr. Newman, and Tompkins, the traumatized survivor of a fiery bomber crash. Tompkins talks to no one and sneaks out every night to the dayroom, where he manages to get drunk on smuggled liquor. Newman and his orderly, Laibowitz, finally get Tompkins to talk, with the assistance of sodium pentathol. Tompkins talks and, through a period of therapy with Dr. Newman, is restored to a measure of sanity, a prospect that haunts Newman in his dreams. If he treats Tompkins effectively, the young man will return to battle and almost certain death. The paradox of his job is that he cures men so they can go out and die. Tompkins goes back to the front. Two months later he dies in a burning Flying Fortress. Newman, anguished, must go on and meet new patients.

Yet another Psychiatric Ward is visited in George Dickerson's "Chico" (1963; *Phoenix*, Spring 1962). In this story, a man (Tommy), has been placed in a naval psychiatric unit. It is written in the first person and in a confused, rambling style invoking the thought processes of one mentally ill. The story features the typical cast of characters found in such stories (see *One Flew Over the Cuckoo's Nest*), but the main character is Chico, a 5' 3" marine veteran of Korea, and the winner of the Congressional Medal of Honor. Chico, much beloved by the men in the ward, sleeps under his bed, and this is a constant point of friction between him and the corpsmen. Chico responds to a command to make his bed, by pointing out, in broken English, that he sleeps on the floor to protect himself from the North Koreans.

Chico loves simple things, like the cream in his tube of shaving cream, which he squeezes gently and watches in delight as the cream squeezes in and out. Chico has found a small tree, no bigger than a foot high, in the exercise yard. He loves the tree and makes it clear to everyone that it is his tree. Unfortunately, a new inmate, a marine called "Junglebunny," appreciates neither Chico nor his tree. He ridicules Chico and calls him a dog because he sleeps under the bed. One day Chico is sent to solitary for a time, and, when he returns, Junglebunny has destroyed his tree. A riot ensues. Later, Tommy helps Chico bury his tree. Chico presides over the funeral like a priest.

Days later, Chico comes to Tommy and tells him he is going to die. Tommy tells him that he won't, but knows better. Somehow, Tommy has gotten the sense that Chico is Jesus Christ, a concern he discusses with Specs, the psychiatrist. Specs tells him that if Chico were Christ, he wouldn't be there, in flesh and blood, unless it were Judgment Day. Chico dies that night. After Chico's funeral, Tommy begins to feel better. He thinks he may be ready to leave the ward. Chico's death reintroduces the theme of military casualties as a type of redemptive sacrifice. Others die so that some may live. Others suffer for the good of all.

Robert O. Bowen's "A Matter of Price" (1955; *Prairie Schooner*, 1954) takes us to another institution and yet another sacrifice, in a veterans' hospital, and to a man who is all too sane. Carson, a veteran of World War II and Korea, has sustained wounds to his shoulder and neck that have left him with nerve damage so bad that the pain robs him of all strength. His surface wounds are healing, but the nerves are damaged beyond repair. His physician, Kimmell, tells him that he has never seen anyone in his condition survive longer than 9 days. Carson has survived for two months, but his condition is degenerative. Drugs provide minimal relief; Carson has refused a lobotomy that could block out the part of the mind affected by pain. Kimmell gives Carson two to four years to live. He is often an exhibit for other physicians at the VA hospital, who come to observe his wounds and dogged survival. During the visits by the other physicians Carson comes to hate the men who treat him as part of a routine, a hatred he realizes he gained during his wartime experiences. The hatred has helped keep him alive. He realizes too that he had had the same clinical attitude displayed by the physicians about killing. He realizes that he had come to enjoy killing and that, initially, he had never looked at it as killing people, but just numbers:

> In Europe that element of action had been a numb thing, firing on a target, always *the target*. In his mind he had never recognized it *man*, and with the others in his squad, gabbing, he phrased it *one*. "I got that one." . . . .
> In Korea the last several men he killed he had watched fall and cease, and once, taking a loner in a little draw, had let him come closer to within ten yards of his bush so he could get the full kick of smashing the guts out of him.[5]

Months of conscious endurance of acute pain has given him much time to ponder things like killing and war:

> The Korean thing had not been a war that he could take pride in or find order in. . . . They killed gooks and they helped gooks. He had not liked World War II for itself, but it had been needful to wipe out the Nazis. . . . In Korea he had held no such constancy. . . . The commies up north were bad, but they weren't Nazi-bad so far as he could judge, and he felt no deep faith in the rightness of him fighting them. . . . Carson felt lost among it all, killing and dying purposely, evilly.[6]

The Korean malaise was best exemplified by a Turkish soldier he had met who proudly showed Carson a tobacco pouch he had made from the skin of a North Korean soldier. Carson could find no purpose in the action, or in the war. It was fought by "Hard men in a hard land, and he among them." As he lay in his hospital bed, enduring the pain, Carson wondered if the chaos of Korea would escalate, or perhaps "like the Turk's tobacco pouch, it would one time come to be a curio to men, harmless of reprisal, abstracted from the past and dried of a living warmth and pain, resting, almost forgot, in an enduring calm. A time when men might cease to kill, when men might think and war be a matter for scholars only."[7]

Carson is ultimately discharged, his flesh healed, but his nerves debilitated. Dr. Kimmell tells Carson he is glad that he did not choose the lobotomy. Carson replies that it did not seem to him the right thing to do. The physician agrees: "Yes . . . . Pain isn't the worse thing in the world."[8] Carson's decision to endure the pain will come into sharp contrast with the Marine depicted in Thom Jones' "The Pugilist at Rest," some forty years later.

The number of stories set in institutions speaks not only to the aftermath of war, but also to a sick society. The problems remaining after and resulting from the war bring to mind an awareness, an anxiety that encourages the impulse to "check out." The option of the lobotomy is tempting. The characters we see are of mixed fates. Some manage to restore their health, some die, but others manage to live through their dysfunction.

# Training Camp

The most interesting of the stories in the post war period are the accounts of various training camps and other stories of routine military life. These types of stories did not appear before 1947, but, between 1947 and 1992, some eight stories are set in training camps. Amidst the typical accounts of sadistic treatment at the hands of their drill instructors are striking revelations about the nature of men and the society's tension between races. While the military has been one of the great levelers of our society, the means of that leveling and the actual "good" of that end, are being questioned.

Philip Garrigan's, "Fly, Fly, Little Dove" (1947; *Atlantic Monthly*, 1946) is a story about a training Camp in Florida, where two homesick "Mexicans" spend most of their off-duty hours in their tent singing and playing mournful songs in Spanish. The Mexicans were always unhappy. The narrator would often pass their tent "and almost always they were sitting on their cots, with all the tent flaps rolled up, conversing loudly and at the same time sadly—for they often wept together, the sound of their voices choked by sobbing."[9] Other soldiers were generally irritated by the music, but a few drunken forays to take the guitar had been met by fierce resistance. The narrator's description of the two men reveals the prejudices of the time:

> The moving pictures had accustomed me to handsome Mexicans. But these two were not so; they were ugly in the sense that they did not look like the rest of us. Short and squat, they had round heads, high cheekbones, and protruding lips. Their noses were flattened, their faces closer to black than to olive, and their hair, coarse and unruly. On the back of Juan's neck it flowed over the collar in a jagged line of bristles. Francisco's mouth was open on a thick tongue and yellowed teeth, some of them broken.[10]

At one point Francisco becomes ill, after a prolonged, unreported illness, and is taken away. He dies later that night. His buddy, Juan, is beside himself with grief. He takes Francisco's guitar, fills it with grass and toilet paper and sets it on fire. Juan gathers up all his worldly possessions and walks away: ". . . behind him the guitar spat and crackled in the flames, and each string as its supports were burned out cried harshly once and for the last time."[11] As Juan tries to walk out of the camp, guards tries to subdue him peacefully. Ultimately, he is clubbed senseless. Life goes on at the camp. The striking thing about this story is just how much the "Mexicans" are outsiders. Language, music, physical appearance, even emotions, set them apart from their fellow soldiers. Not only are their differences ignored, but those differences lead ultimately to their deaths.

Life and death are again an issue in Wyatt Blassingame's "Man's Courage" (1957; *Harper's*, 1956), another story which addresses racial tensions. In this case, Lieutenant Henderson, an African-American, is engaged in a battle of wills with Private Lee Stewart, a white Mississippian. Henderson and Stewart had been at odds throughout their time together at the training camp. Henderson had been a victim of repeated disrespect and Stewart repeated punishment for lack of the same. The story is told from the perspective of one of the veterans in the airborne unit, which had fought with distinction in World War II and Korea. The general perspective, among the men, was that Henderson was weak. He was the first Negro officer under whom the men had served and Stewart voiced an un- spoken sentiment among them: that a black man did not belong in their unit. Henderson, immediately aware of Stewart's resentment and troublemaking, had Stewart serve as his driver for trips into town. When Henderson had Stewart go into a segregated bar and purchase him a bottle of whiskey, Stewart had been taunted by the barmaid about his connection to the black officer. At that point Private Stewart vows to kill Henderson.

Shortly thereafter, on the night before maneuvers, Stewart had stayed late at the bar, past the midnight curfew. The next morning he was back at the barracks, telling a story with an amused incredulity. Stewart had walked back to the post around two a.m. and was preparing to find a way to sneak over the fence when he encountered Henderson, armed with a pistol. Henderson confronts Stewart with a rumor that one of the men is planning to kill him. He tells Stewart that he'll need a bodyguard, hands him the gun, and orders him to follow him back into camp, three paces behind, so that he won't be shot in the back. They walked on that way until they reached the gate to the camp. Henderson turned to Stewart and asked him why he didn't kill him when he had the chance. Stewart re- sponded that he couldn't shoot a man, even a black one, in the back. He then realizes that Henderson had given him the gun to prove to him that he was not a coward. Henderson points out he had to prove it to the unit as well. He had to squelch the insubordination. Henderson assigns Stewart to KP duty for being out after curfew. Stewart responds with the customary "yes sir," the first he has given to Henderson.

Later, the confused Stewart attempts to explain the incident to the men back at the barracks. A person of Henderson's race wouldn't have known Stewart couldn't shoot him in the back, so he still deserved the respect implied by "sir." Stewart's confusion and ultimate resolution represent much of the national mindset at the time. The struggle between white and black is subordinated to a larger principle. One may not have his or her heart in an applied local example, but may be moved by the principle, in this case, the good of the regiment and Army discipline.

More racial tensions, this time regarding Jews, appear in Philip Roth's "The Defender of the Faith" (1960; *New Yorker*, 14 March 1959). The story is set in the closing days of World War II. Sergeant Nathan Marx, the story's narrator, a veteran of the war in Europe is assigned to a training camp in Missouri. There, among the trainees in his platoon, are three young Jewish soldiers from New

York City, Grossbart, Fishbein, and Halpern. Grossbart, realizes his new sergeant is Jewish and approaches him about being excused from Friday night barracks cleaning to attend services. Though the men are technically excused, it is felt that their peers might think it strange that they be excused, unless some official intervention occurs. Marx approaches his Captain on the issue and receives little encouragement. On Friday afternoon, however, Marx has the Charge of Quarters read an announcement indicating that recruits may attend worship services, whenever they are held. Marx follows the three men to services and notices that they seem to be less than attentive.

Next, Grossbart makes an issue of the food, which is non kosher. He even writes a letter for his immigrant (and non English speaking) father to mail to their Congressman. Marx sniffs out this plot, only to be addressed by another. One of the three has a relative in St. Louis, who will prepare them a Seder. The problem is that recruits are not allowed passes. Marx remembers that Passover had passed weeks before. Grossbart responds indignantly that his aunt will be going to a lot of trouble to make them a special Passover meal. Ultimately, it turns out that the three men visited no relative, and attended no Seder. Nonetheless, Marx performs one more favor. Grossbart has asked him to find out where the recruits will be shipped after training. As a kindness, Marx inquires and finds out the men will be shipped to Germany. He tells Grossbart. Later, when official orders arrive, he finds all the men will be shipped to Japan except Grossbart. Grossbart is to be shipped to Monmouth, New Jersey. Marx figures out that Grossbart has pulled a string and has the orders changed. Marx pulls strings of his own. Grossbart will go to the Pacific with the others.

Grossbart confronts Marx and the two engage in an animated discussion. Marx, the higher ranking man, wins. The story closes with Marx standing outside the barracks where Grossbart sits weeping. The men polish their shoes and brass, coming to grips with their fate. Marx himself wonders whether he has crossed a line in getting back at Grossbart. Marx is torn between what constitutes harassment against his own race and what constitutes good military discipline. In the end he knows he is manipulated by Grossbart. The question remains, however: Was his vindictiveness aimed to serve the better good of the Army, or was it he playing what George Garrett called the "Old Army Game?"

"The Old Army Game "(1962; *Sewanee Review*, July-September 1961) is another story about the brutality of basic training and chickenshit. The training camp depicted here is run by cruel men who have no regard for anyone. The reader is left to ponder how productive such a system can be. Can the Army be changed, or must it always change the man? This is a first person narrative with occasional interjections by a self conscious writer. Sergeant Quince is the drill instructor who makes it clear he likes no one. He is so ornery that he drills the men through the much prized garden of his superior, Sergeant Cobb, a tired veteran of World War I. Cobb is so cowed by Quince's bluster that he will not voice a protest. Garrett, the writer, is conscious that he is writing what may be interpreted as the stereotypical account of a brutal drill sergeant. He realizes, he writes, that he is supposed to tell us about some of the sergeant's personal background before moving on. So, he tells us of the misadventures of him and his fellow misfits and just how cruel and sadistic Quince was in whipping them into shape. Again, Garrett knows his reader has heard it before, but moves on.

They all survive basic, but, as they are packing to leave for their new assignments, old Sergeant Cobb trudges into the barracks. He tells the men that Sergeant Quince's wife has been in a bad accident and is dying. Quince was broke and needed cash to go home to see about his wife and family. Cobb asks the men to donate some money. After a period of silence, one man comes forward and drops a solitary dime into the helmet liner that serves as the pot. Each man then comes forward, depositing his own dime. Sergeant Cobb laughed in astonishment. It seems that the men in the other barracks had done the same thing. Thirty minutes later they see Quince, standing out in the rain in the battery area. He curses the men and angrily throws the dimes into the sky. Again, Garrett, the writer, breaks in to the story and tells the reader that he knows that the story is now supposed to end, but that he must tell more.

The narrator and Sachs, one of his fellow survivors, are assigned to Leadership School, in part, they hope, to become the opposite of Quince. They succeed, are promoted to sergeants themselves, and are assigned to Germany, rather than Korea. About a year after training camp, whom should they encounter in Germany, but Quince, now busted to Corporal, and looking the antithesis of his former spit and polish self. They buy Quince a beer and spend the evening with him as if they were old buddies. Eventually, when Quince has become drunk and crying in his beer, he confronts the two men. He tells the new sergeants that he had hated them long before the incident with the dimes, but that he didn't know that they hated him so much that they would track him down in the bar and buy him drinks to shame him. The Army, he says, is his life, but that they are only in it for a few years and now they come in showing off their rank and acting like soldiers. Sachs tells Quince that the Army is a silly game. Moreover, he tells Quince, he has won the game. He'll be a better soldier than Quince. Quince turns his head away, telling him that he should not have said that. The narrator congratulates Sachs for putting Quince in his place. Sachs responds angrily. No, he says, Quince won in the end. Quince forced him to respond as he did. Nobody wins the old Army game except the army itself.

Ivan Gold's "The Nickel Misery of George Washington Carver Brown" (1961; *Esquire*, March 1960) is set in yet another integrated training camp, but this time with a vortex of dysfunctionality begat by both the chickenshit of army life and the complex intricacies of race. George Washington Carver Brown is a large, black, clumsy, dimwitted recruit, who had been the butt of every unfortunate incident in camp. Roger Hines is a frail, college-educated, light-skinned Northern Negro who had made no friend in camp and was particularly bristly to those who tried to befriend him. Hines is particularly contemptuous of Brown, whom he mentally refers to as a fool. Brown, for his part, is somewhat contemptuous of Hines, to whom he refers as Copperhead. Hines tells Brown that his name is Roger and that he will not respond to names based on the color of his skin. Carver responds, telling him that the nickname has nothing to do with his color, but because his face looks like that of a snake. The conversation takes place while the men are seated inches away at the toilets, performing bodily functions Hines would rather perform in private. He hates Brown because he sees him as a living example of everything he had been raised not to be.

A third recruit is Frazier, a white southerner, who had developed progressive attitudes toward race relations after being expelled from his college fraternity for dating a black woman. Frazier regarded the harassment of Brown as motivated only incidentally by race. From his point of view, training camp has been uniformly cruel to men of all colors and creeds. Brown, in his mind, was simply a misfit. Frazier, on the other hand, eagerly seeks to make friends with Hines. He invites him to join him for a weekend visit to Atlanta. Hines, who now regards Frazier as his worst enemy, replies witheringly that he is a Negro and has no desire to find out what things are like in Atlanta. Frazier replies that he though Hines might be interested on learning about the racial situation in Atlanta. He goes on in an attempt to show Hines how progressive he is on racial matters. He earnestly wants to know about Hines' life, his background. Hines could care less, telling him he has no interest in the racial situation and would rather not be patronized.

Confounding the daily struggles of the three recruits, are Corporal Cherry and Sergeant Divino, both wounded veterans of the Korean War, and their Captain, Palmer. Palmer is oblivious to the struggles of the enlisted men and Cherry enjoys tormenting the men sadistically. Divino, who refers to all recruits derogatorily in an attempt to be egalitarian, vows to leave the service because he can deal with either Cherry or Palmer, but not with both at the same time.

The story reaches its climax on the obstacle course, where Cherry has forced Brown to climb to the top of a ladder with five foot wide rungs. Hines, who had suffered from a broken ankle earlier in training, and is excused from the exercise, watched peacefully beneath the shade of a pine tree. Frazier had preceded Brown over the obstacle with a contemptuous whoop. Brown, making it to the top, freezes on one of the rungs, and Cherry climbs up and carries him down. Cherry then forces Brown to climb it again. The others look on with a variety of emotions, Divino second guessing Cherry's strategy, Frazier seeing the action as racially motivated, and Hines wondering what they're going to do to Brown. Brown climbs again, struggling, and falls, breaking his back on a hurdle, and slicing open his face on coiled barbed wire. Divino strikes Cherry in the face and throat with his fists. Frazier looks around frantically for Hines, wondering if this event gets a sympathetic reaction.

Gold's training camp is a microcosm of American racial tensions: dissent and prejudice between African-Americans, the rejected and perhaps misguided intentions of whites, and the ever present motif of the military experience, humiliation. One is left to ask whether the military experience eliminates the differences between us, or does it reinforce them? Or does the military care?

While Roth and Gold address racial and ethnic tensions in training camp, the romance of the Civil War returns, but with a twist fitting the postwar era. Phyllis Roberts' "Hero" (1960; *Virginia Quarterly Review*, Spring 1959) is cast as an old man's reminiscence of a boyhood memory, when Civil War veterans still marched through towns in yearly commemoration of the war. In this case, the veterans are from the Confederate Army. The boy's father, a former officer on Lee's staff, frowns on the yearly gatherings, as does the son in his adult hindsight. The men camped on the outskirts of town, raised cane for a week, and paraded through the town in faded uniforms. The young boy thinks it all terribly romantic. The boy's father tries to put it all into perspective, pointing out that the group was composed of mortal men.

In the incident described, the seven-year-old boy is watching the parade and is swept up into the arms of a dashing veteran, Ace Kane. Kane carries him astride his great Arabian stallion to the encampment. There, the young boy revels in the excitement of being with the ex-soldiers. Eventually, the boy is taken home to dinner, where his mother invites Kane to stay for dinner. Kane charms the women of the family and, to the boy's surprise, engages his father with some shared war experiences. Kane departs for the night and returns the following afternoon to take the boy on a glorious exploration of a former battlefield, where they find Minié balls beneath the water of a bubbling spring. Kane and the other veterans depart that evening, though the boy knows he will see him again.

Later, on a September night, the boy is awakened by a barking dog and a disturbance in the yard. Rushing to the window, he sees his father's fine red stallion, fully saddled, and rushing about frantically as three men fight: his father, the family servant, Dart, and a masked man. The boy rushed into the yard to witness his father efficiently beat the masked horse thief to the ground. The boy rushes to his father, who tries to send him back to the house. The boy looks to the bloody face of the thief, whose masked had slipped to reveal the face of Ace Kane. The father takes the heartbroken boy into his arms and tells Dart to present the stallion to Kane, as his gift, from a fellow veteran. The boy clings to his father, as his view of the world is altered forever. He now knew that the world was populated by men not gods. This story, though cast in a romantic light, presents a revised view of the hero, with feet of clay. Heroism is a mask that can easily slip to reveal a human face.

By 1960 popular music had begun to project social messages. Joan Baez cut her first album in 1960 and was on the charts throughout the decade as she became involved in the civil rights and anti-war movements. Bob Dylan appeared on the scene in 1962 and was also a continued presence. Barry McGuire recorded "Eve of Destruction" in 1965, summarizing the turbulent mood in the country, and a year later a soldier named Barry Sadler recorded "The Ballad of the Green Beret." John Wayne starred in a film by the same name in 1968. Kenny Rogers scored a hit in 1969 with a song, written by country musician, Mel Tillis, "Ruby, Don't Take Your Love to Town," that referred to a "crazy Asian war." Merle Haggard endeared himself to conservative America with

"Okie from Muscogee." The Woodstock festival was a big event of 1969 and an independent, countercultural film called "Easy Rider" became a hit.

Meanwhile, as the war in Vietnam escalated, 1968 featured a pair of stories describing rites of passage in the military from World War II and before. Leo E. Litwik's "In Shock" (*Partisan Review*, Fall 1968) and Richard McKenna's "The Sons of Martha" (*Harper's*, February 1967) McKenna's "The Sons of Martha" is an even greater anachronism, chronicling life in the pre World War II Navy.

Reed Kinburn has transferred onto a supply ship from a job as a corpsman in a naval hospital. He had to transfer or be discharged after Roosevelt had ordered veterans removed from the naval hospitals. He was supporting his mother and younger brothers with an allotment from his meager pay. The Navy provided a job, food and shelter in an America deep in the Depression. As a new man he draws duty cleaning the combustion chambers of the ship's boiler, a gritty, filthy job that requires him to chip out carbon, inch by inch, with a chisel. The job takes him deep into the night and he emerges from the engine room black with soot. He stands in the shower puzzling as to how he might ever get clean. Horgan, the water tender first class, comes to the shower room with a loofa, soap, and hot water in a pail. He shows Kinburn how to clean himself with suds from the bucket, using the same filthy water over and over. Kinburn emerges from the shower, dingy gray, but clean. Horgan tells him that the gray will just have to wear off. Horgan tells him that he has done the work of three men. He tells him to sleep late, take the next day off, and that plenty of beer is waiting for him ashore, courtesy of Horgan. When Kinburn retires to his cot and drifts toward sleep he experience rest like he had not experienced in a while. The bitterness has been replaced by the satisfaction of having finished hard work.

Litwik's story, written in the first person, is an account of a young man, Anthony, who has been drafted out of college to train as a medic during World War II. Anthony feels ill suited to be a medic; his bandages are clumsy and his injections cause bruising. He is the subject of ridicule from his sergeant. He is one of only two college men in his training class; the other Joe Witty, a capable premed student from Michigan, is the star of the class. Another factor in Anthony's discomfort is a sense of sexual inadequacy. He believes the other men think he is queer. He fails in his attempts to utilize the services from a local bordello, where all the other men have gone. It doesn't help matters that the only acquaintance Anthony has in camp is Jason, a college classmate, who hangs with a group of men regarded by the others as sexually suspect and serves as a clerk. Jason feels sure that he can get Anthony transferred to be a clerk. Anthony resists, feeling he has to be connected with combat.

All Anthony's attempts at manly competence seem futile. Witty menaces him in the shower and another man head butts him on the obstacle course. The sergeant assigns him additional KP. He seriously considers the transfer to clerk at Headquarters. He still resists, because he fears he will become homosexual. After much deliberation, he challenges Wittty to a boxing match. The match ends in a draw, but Anthony feels the loser because Witty's punches drew blood. Dejected, he seeks out Jason and his friends in the music room of the USO, where they are playing the *Liebestod*. He asks Jason to arrange his transfer.

The next day Anthony is biding his time on duty at the rifle range when the cry goes out for a medic. Reluctantly, he is rushed to the site of a dynamite explosion, where a man's leg has been blown off his body. He ties a clumsy tourniquet, injects morphine, and with a great deal of difficulty, manages to cover the wound as the man is rushed to the hospital. He does not even leave the hospital before his life changes. The ambulance driver tells him that he performed well. The Commanding Officer praises him. By the time he returns to his battalion, he is a hero. With new found confidence, he tells Witty he is ready for a rematch. Witty puts him off. Suddenly, Witty wants to be Anthony's friend. When Anthony persists, Witty apologizes to him in front of the other men and shakes his hand. He sees now that Witty is no different from himself. Anthony realizes that he has made it, but he still feels no different. Like many things to which we aspire and seem to be so difficult, the actual attainment is a disappointment. In the general scheme of things, what had Anthony accomplished? Underneath he was the same insecure person.

Jules Siegel's "In the Land of the Morning Calm, Déjà vu," (1970; *Esquire*, 1969) takes us back to Korea with a tale that features homoeroticism amidst a certain amount of gore. Frazer, an army photographer, has a recurring dream, which is revealed at the opening of the story. Frazer sees himself, naked, at a beach with another man and an officer approaching them. The story then proceeds to detail Frazer's early duties as a photographer. A truce is in progress, but there are plenty of grisly crime scenes, suicides, and accidents for him to photograph. He wonders if there could be more dead bodies during hostilities. Soon, however, Frazer is transferred to a military intelligence unit in Seoul. He was to be deployed for occasional aerial reconnaissance photography. He quickly becomes friends with Remsen, a translator from Iowa.

The dynamic in his new unit is strange. He witnesses a South Korean interrogation of a double agent, who is cruelly tortured. The man is brought in, wearing only shorts. The reaction of his coworkers changes. They watch the man intently while breathing heavily. The scene reminds him of the atmosphere at a peep show. After witnessing the incident, Frazer begins to have his recurring dream.

Frazer and Remsen are tent mates, and they enjoy amorous relations with Korean prostitutes, though Frazer observes that Remsen seems somewhat detached from his women after the sex act is completed. Later, Remsen is shot when investigating a crime scene. Frazer is lonely during his friend's recuperation and is puzzled when a sergeant observes that Remsen would be better off out of the army, that he was a section eight candidate.

Remsen returns from the hospital at the height of summer. The men sleep naked in their steamy tent and one night Frazer wakes to find Remsen gazing at him intently. Later that day they decide to go to a beach that is forbidden for military personnel. They enjoy their time at the beach, swimming in the cool water. Frazer bemoans the fact that they brought no women with them. Remsen replies by asking Frazer if he ever gets tired of women. Frazer asks if there is something else. Remsen looks at him knowingly and suggests he knows. Frazer replies negatively, but knows something is about to happen. At this point Frazer's nightmare becomes reality as the Lieutenant approaches the two naked men on the beach.

It is interesting that as stories of Vietnam still wait to be told and the controversy of "Don't ask, Don't tell" is twenty five years away, two stories treat, at least peripherally, the issue of gay soldiers. That theme, however, does not resurface for some thirty-six years.

The transformational value of the military experience was depicted in another story, Andre Dubus' "Cadence" (1975; *Sewanee Review*, Summer 1974). "Cadence" is another coming of age story about training camp, this time Marine Officer's Candidate School in Quantico, Virginia. Remarkably for this era, the story features no reference to race. There is a brief reference to one of the character's, Paul's, breakup with a girlfriend because of his Catholicism. Paul, the protagonist is an undersized 19 year old from Louisiana, who is goaded and pummeled from his first day in camp. From that first day he wants to go home, but he can't bring himself to see the shame on his father's face when he returns. His size puts him at a disadvantage, particularly in running and marching, where he struggles to keep up with the other, longer legged, men. He and his bunkmate, Hugh Munson, worked together in learning to read maps and prepare their equipment. Hugh is as physically challenged as Paul in many respects, and they provide each other moral support and a sounding board. Eventually, the drill sergeant, Hathaway, pits the two against each other. After Paul successfully beats Hugh in a drill with pugil sticks, Hugh mutters that he thinks Paul must be enjoying himself. Paul ignores Hugh's comment.

Now comes a grueling march at night, through the hills. Paul and Hugh are both spent when the Lieutenant commands them to march again. Paul quickly falls to the back of the pack. Two other men hold him up by the arms and tell him that he can do it. Eventually, though, Paul stumbles to the gravel. Hathaway gives him water and helps him up and commands him to press on. After a wobbly start Paul gains his stride and knows he will make it. Hathaway and Paul stop again at the limp body of Hugh, who has vomited in the ditch. Hathaway urges Hugh to go on with them, but Hugh refuses, saying he can't. They leave Hugh behind and, breaking through another wave of fatigue, Paul finds new strength in his legs. When they join the other recruits, Hathaway leads Paul on a half-mile run around the parade ground. He returns to the barracks and prepares wearily for bed. The next morning Hugh does not get out of bed with the others. He finally falls in to the formation, unshaven, and is summarily chewed out by Hathaway. Hugh says he is going home. He walks away, ignoring the rest of Hathaway's screams. Hathaway instructs the men to ignore Hugh's presence at breakfast. He marches them to the mess hall chanting in cadence that they will not talk to or look at Hugh. Later that day, as Paul fills in the hole Hugh has left in the file, he experienced a feeling of certainty.

Dubus' story could have been written at any time in the twentieth century. It captures the struggle people have in stretching themselves to the limits of their endurance. It could have been written about athletes. The remarkable thing here is that it is a relatively uncritical account of the whole affair. Unlike so many of the training camp accounts we have seen since World War II, it simply presents the ordeal as just another challenge that must be overcome. It seems ever rarer when contrasted with the bleak, fatalistic accounts of the war in Vietnam.

Preceding the first wave of stories about Vietnam is a domestic account of the cold war in Joseph Whitehall's "One Night for Several Samurai" (1966; *Hudson Review*, Summer 1965). The story centers around Moyama, a Japanese born university professor, his senior colleague, Graves, a physicist, and Bales, a major in the United States Air Force. Moyama, who had served in the Japanese military, as a teenager, during World War II, and was destined to be a kamikaze pilot until the war had ended, has done research, supported in part by funding from the Air Force. He has published part of his research in an academic journal. Graves is intrigued with the measurement of a certain phenomenon reported in the article and has dropped by Moyama's living quarters several times to discuss it. He is particularly interested in a measuring device. Moyama tells him that the Air Force will not permit him to disclose the information, but Graves persists in asking at each visit. On the rainy night in which the story is set Moyama has alerted Bales of another visit by Graves and contrived a way for Bales to stop by Moyama's apartment.

As colleagues do, Moyama and Graves talk about a variety of subjects. One topic is Moyama's former destiny as a kamikaze. Graves has always been puzzled by the issue and the two men probe it intellectually. Graves wonders if Moyama believed that death as a kamikaze would have been glorious. Moyama concedes that he probably did. They move to Moyama's research and then to the "sensitive" issue which Moyama will not discuss. Graves cannot believe that Moyama can work in an environment where ideas cannot be fully exchanged. Moyama is incredulous that Graves cannot conceive of powers and causes greater than himself. Graves replies that he knows that there are forces, like the government, that are more powerful, but that he had to be a free man. Moyama replies that he just concentrates on his work. Graves responds that that is the trouble. He then invokes examples of Nazi medical experiments, nuclear physicist and V-2 rocket scientists to support his case. Moyama responds by putting the situation in perspective. He points out how twenty years before he was immersed in a culture that viewed the U. S. as an evil entity out to enslave Asia; that Pearl Harbor was a defensive attack. Now he is an American and does what his country asks him as a citizen. Graves concedes that he may be a bad citizen, but that he is a free man who relies on reason. Moyama retorts that much evil has been done under the name of reason. At this point their conversation is interrupted by Major Bales and a lady friend, who arrive under the guise of a social call. Graves rises to leave and Bales, rather forcefully, insists on driving him

home on such a rainy night. Rather than take Graves directly home, Bales takes
a circuitous route that leads them on a dark road out of town. The major initiates
a discussion that implies that Graves is a spy. He tells Graves that he probably
isn't a "big traitor," but just an "innocent dupe." Graves wonders how to outfox
Bales. He realizes that the key is Bales' career ambitions. He reminds Bales that
he did not get as far as he had in his career by taking action independent of his
superiors. He further implies that Bales' superiors might not be pleased if told of
his actions. Graves, having dealt with Bales on his own level, is soon taken
home.

Though set early in the Vietnam era, this story sets the lines seen so clearly
as domestic protests against the war begin: loyal, unquestioning Americans versus those opposed to military and foreign policy. Whitehall uses the specter of
the Japanese totalitarian state held up against our own in a chilling, critical way.

# Vietnam and Beyond

Vietnam finally makes an entrance in the series with two rather arresting
stories by John Bart Gerald in 1969 and 70. "Walking Wounded" (*Harper's*,
August, 1968) opens in the chapel of an Air Force base, where our protagonist,
Dunbar, the story's narrator works as a medical specialist, evacuating wounded
troops, fresh from Vietnam, to the base hospital. Though not personally involved
in combat, he is touched by it every day. Soldiers tell him stories, like the one
about the Vietnamese woman who tried to lure a soldier into her booby trapped
hut. He spots the trip wire and refuses to go in: "'Her dress was open. I pushed
her off and shot her up the front. Then I took off a grenade and rolled it smooth
through the front door of her hut and blew out two kids. I didn't mind the woman so much.'"[12]

Though he has never forgotten the story, he now concedes that it has come
to bore him a little. He has heard too many stories. He doesn't like the war, but
he doesn't hate it either. He has become something of a fatalist and views the
military and the world in pretty bleak terms: "You make scratch or you get
rubbed out. We're all part of one great machine."[13] Going to church, marching
in parades, and tending the wounded are his part of the machine.

He gives us a glimpse of a day's work, unloading the wounded, screaming,
moaning, still in bandages applied on the battlefield. His job is to remove the
puss soaked dressings, clean the wounds, and apply fresh bandages. One man
threatens to kill him if he touches his wounds any more. Another man, a young
black man, whose leg has been amputated, tells him that if he gets orders to go
overseas, he should refuse: "'Don't go, man.' He said it again and I thought he
was being political, trying to sell me something. 'Don't go,' he kept saying. Until I realized that was what he had to tell me, like the other guys had their war
stories, it was the only thing he knew anymore."[14]

He walks into another ward, where he encounters an unscathed soldier with a case of shell shock. The man tells him that he has come to "hate too much." Dunbar responds that hate "is no simple thing."[15] The man proceeds to tell Dunbar how they used to cut off the ears of the enemy, how they had found one of their men, hung up by his feet, still alive, with his "things" stuffed in his mouth. After being cut down, the mutilated soldier asks to be shot and their sergeant complies. Dunbar extracts himself from the conversation. As he walks away he mentally dismisses the man's story as an old one, routinely told in basic training. Still, he muses, "the kid must have done something nasty to be pushing it around as his own, that kid with his body still whole and strong. That means a lot where I work."[16]

Dunbar's shift finally ends and he goes home, showers, and falls into bed with his wife. He hugs his wife to his body and realizes that he still can smell the putrid scent of old wounds. He pulls away from her and sits naked, on the edge of the bed, looking at his body: "Because that's all I have left. I am alive. I'm breathing."[17] The focus on war and the military experience has changed sharply. No longer is it merely the training experience presented as brutal and harsh, but so is war itself. No longer is the art of killing seen as destruction of an enemy alone, but of destruction to ourselves. It is perhaps an apt description of the Viet Nam era.

Gerald's second story, "Blood Letting" (*Atlantic*, May 1969) is directly related to the first, even appropriating the same line from "a black man without legs who looked in my eyes and said, 'Don't go.'"[18] This story, though, only features Viet Nam on its periphery. It opens with a vivid, shocking paragraph. A soldier, Blake, shows up in his Colonel's office, out of uniform and asks to show him something. Blake then proceeds to carve a bloody cross into his own chest:

> With an edge cutting in my hand I pulled the blade down the middle of my chest through the T-shirt and hair down to the bone. And as the blood sprang into the split flesh I drew another cut across the top of my chest to make a cross. And stood there with the warm seeping down into my pants, looking at him, realizing he would never see me, or any of us.[19]

The story then proceeds, in the first person, to provide a personal narrative of Blake's life. The son of a successful businessman, he attends Harvard, but drops out for a time to work with Dr. Schweitzer, caring for lepers. Returning to Harvard, he symbolically crosses out his name where it appears in his club's historic membership book. After graduation he joins the Air Force Reserve, marries, and gets a job teaching school. He feels uncomfortable with his life. The summation of his discomfort is presented in periodic style:

> It was awkward to feel that the war starting was immoral and would ultimately be disastrous to the people of the country, and to belong at the same time to the military. It was awkward teaching that stories and ideals were as real as life's blood when some of my students would graduate into war. It was awkward paying taxes. It was awkward distrusting my government. I found a number of

things awkward. What amazed me was how much awkwardness I could live with.[20]

He marched in peace demonstrations and for civil rights, but carefully bifurcated his life. He refused to advise his students who asked whether they should go to jail to avoid military service. He himself deeply fears military prisons. He wanted to believe that his life was heroic, yet he realizes that he "preferred heroism without having to pay too much too often."[21] He reminds himself that he has a choice to follow his conscience, yet he fears putting his conscience to the test.

There were reports that his reserve unit would be called to active duty. Flight to Canada was an option, but he realizes that he is an American, "no great patriot but the country was a part of myself. I couldn't ignore it. I couldn't resign from my whole life. I couldn't resign from myself."[22] He thinks of his experiences in Africa, of the march in Selma, of a comforting boyhood moment with his father, when he'd told him he'd be all right. He thought of the Lord's Prayer. His wife knows that something is about to happen. She stands crying by their bed. He has made up his mind: "When I was ready I hugged her as strong as I could but I didn't feel her. There was a knot tied in my chest pulling tighter and tighter and tighter. I said, "See you." And when I walked out the door I fell into America."[23] The America he falls into is schizophrenic, dysfunctional, and suicidal. Yet, there is an overly of Christian spirituality here that has rarely been seen in stories since the Great War.

James S. Kenary's "Going Home," (1973; *Massachusetts Review*, 1973) continues the thread from Vietnam. This story is about a young man, Will, who has sustained a combat wound that he hopes will send him home from Vietnam. He is treated in a field hospital, where medics and nurses rush about treating the wounded men. One of his friends, Ben, is seriously wounded and wheeled into surgery. Another man, unknown to him, is dying on a table nearby. He waits for his turn in X-ray as the man next to him breathes his last. Will feels a little neglected in the hustle and bustle of the hospital, but he consoles himself that he is going home.

A nurse covers him with a blanket and talks with him for a while. Her brother had died in the war. They both hope the war will end soon. She washes his wound and prepares his leg for the doctor, who will try to remove shrapnel from his wound. One of his buddies, Bart, is wheeled by. The nurse tells him that Bart's leg has been amputated.

The nurse finishes her work and leaves him for the doctor. Alone, he fantasizes how the doctor will tell him he is going home. Will waits for a long time. The doctor comes, finally, and begins to probe his wound roughly. The doctor finishes his probing and Will waits for the announcement. The shrapnel is still in the wound. It may work its way out, or it may never come out. The doctor writes up something in his chart and slaps Will on his good leg, telling him that he was ready to return to his unit. Will is shocked. He is not going home. He limps to the doorway of the hospital and is met by his lieutenant and top sergeant. He limps slowly to the bright light of the doorway. He knows he will be back in the war and drops to the floor, sobbing uncontrollably.

In yet another story that offers a critique of the war, Ward Just's "Dietz at War" (1976; *Virginia Quarterly Review*, 1975) tells an almost allegorical story about a war correspondent, presumably assigned to Vietnam, who becomes lost in a personal fantasy of the war. His fantasy, in many ways, seems to mime the vision of the government at the time. In addition to regular dispatches to his paper, Dietz also sends lengthy weekly letters to his children. The letters home obscure any significant details about his adventures. He intended them for his children, but his ex-wife tells him he is really writing the letters for her. He had friends and lovers in the war zone, but he never revealed any of the details of those relationships to his family.

Dietz has not been home to America in over three years. He prides himself as being totally objective in his reporting of the war. He used irony in his presentation of the facts, however, to portray what he saw as ill conceived actions. He wrote of no atrocities. His goal, rather, was to describe the war in a way fitting Henry James. Dietz works at being authoritative in his reporting of every detail about the war, yet he refuses to learn the country's history, customs, or language. All he knows about the country pertains to the war.

He is encouraged one day to accompany a patrol on a dangerous mission designed to establish enemy presence in a neighboring neutral country. The patrol is ambushed, the officers are killed and a dozen men are wounded, including Dietz. No sanctuaries are found. After five days in the hospital, Dietz first writes a letter to his children and then writes the story for his paper from memory. Upon proofreading he discovers that his command of the facts was poor. He style was different, too. Somehow he had written a relatively cheerful story. His editors loved it. In the years following the ambush he immersed himself in describing details of the country. He frequently played the role of a travel writer and even published fictional information from time to time. The war becomes for Dietz, as well as his readers, an everyday routine.

After five years, Dietz's newspaper wants him to come home; the public no longer cares about the war. But Dietz stays on and risks being fired. The country and the war had become his life and Dietz had totally immersed himself in it. He no longer engaged in a social life and sent letters home that were bland and tedious. He wrote stories, widely viewed as authoritative, but often devoid of fact. Amidst the grim realities of a long war, punctuated by daily body counts, Dietz and the country continue the war for the sake of the war alone.

Meanwhile, the frustrating experience of the actual war continues, as depicted in Tim O'Brien's "Going After Cacciato" (1977; *Ploughshares*, 1976). This story portrays a platoon at a particularly difficult time in the Viet Nam War. Six men have died and the rainy season has set in. The men are ravaged by fungus and dysentery. One day, at the end of October, Cacciato, not regard by anyone as particularly intelligent, goes AWOL. He told one of the men, Berlin, that he was going to Paris. Berlin tells the Lieutenant that Cacciato has taken off with maps and a compass and is going to walk 6, 800 miles to Paris by way of

Laos, Thailand, Burma, India, Iran, Iraq, Turkey, Greece and so forth. He has charted out his route on maps.

The new Lieutenant, Corson, a weary veteran of Korea, busted back to Lieutenant because of drink, and currently suffering from dysentery, leads Third Squad, Cacciato's squad in pursuit of the AWOL soldier. After a half day's walk, they spot him a mile away in the distance. They come across his discarded food containers and maps. The men rest there. One man plays solitaire. Another rolls a joint and passes it around. One man suggests to Corson that they just let him go. Corson disappears into the bushes with a roll of toilet paper. When he comes back he tells the men to proceed with the chase. One of the soldiers, Stink, is pleased with Corson's decision to stay after him: he argues that a man just can't be allowed to walk away from a war.

The men press on, over the mountains. At one point a smiling Cacciato waves at them through the mist they yell at Cacciato and he flaps his arms at them like a bird. He hollers back a fare well. When the men rest for the night, Berlin has a vision of Cacciato being murdered by a bullet to the temple. He wonders where their pursuit will lead them. He knows that death is the inevitable consequence of stupidity in war.

On the third day they lose sight of Cacciato, but they find his dog tags and other equipment, abandoned on the trail. They see him again and then realize that he is now only two kilometers from the border with Laos. They see him again, this time only two hundred meters away. Cacciato waves at them, looking amused. Stink wants to fire a shot at him. Just then the squad trips over a booby trap Cacciato has set for them. They are literally scared to the point of death, but the trap contained only smoke bombs. The message is clear: Cacciato could have had them. Johnson is sent out under a white flag to talk to Cacciato, but he will not come back. The next morning they awake and see Cacciato's breakfast fire in the distance. Berlin wonders why he didn't slip across the border in the night. Corson makes the decision to go after him. The others leave in two groups to capture Cacciato. Berlin is assigned to fire a flare. As the flare illuminates the hillside he whispers and then shouts the command to go after him.

The story captures Vietnam in its most pathetic light. In this case, men caught in a seemingly senseless war are literally sent on a fool's errand, following a fool. Any sense of military discipline is gone. Men freely smoke marijuana and are led by a man struggling with his own survival, much less the survival of his men.

Larry Heinemann, "The First Clean Fact," (1980; *Triquarterly*, 1979) recounts a grim story that is told in conversational style to a man named James. It features a loose, vulgar vernacular that presents almost everything in the crudest fashion: "spooks," "gooks," and "zips," as well as GIs, are "greased" in battle. "Viets" work at their base camp as cashiers and barbers: "And, James, don't you know they were Viets during the day and zips at night (one zip we body-counted one time couldn't booby-trap a shithouse any better than he could cut hair)"

(214). The men are entertained by a troop of Filipino musicians, whose female lead singer excites them to the point of "circle-jerking our brains out."[24]

The narrator knows that no one wants to hear about his company's demise at Landing Zone Skater-Gator, where the whole company, but one, got killed: "Fucked-up dead, James, scarfed up."[25] They were fighting near a village they called "Gookville" when they were hit by "every incoming round left in creation."[26] Very quickly, "everything was transformed into Crispy Critters for half a dozen clicks in any direction . . . "[27] "Oh, we dissolved all right, but our screams burst through the ozone, burst through the rags and tatters and café-looking aurora borealis . . . into God's everlasting Cosmos."[28] "And we're pushing up daisies for half a handful of millennia . . . but that bloodcurdling scream is rattling all over God's ever-loving Creation like a BB in a boxcar, only louder."[29] Again, the soldier in Vietnam realizes the insignificance of his struggle. Here, similar to March's vignettes from the Great War, a dead man tells the tale.

Tim O'Brien's "The Things They Carried" (1987; *Esquire*, 1986) is the poignant account of a platoon in Viet Nam and of their first fatality. Punctuating the account is a litany of the things the men carried with them every day. As the story progresses, the list of baggage progresses from the physical to the emotional. The platoon leader, Lieutenant Jimmy Cross, carries letters and pictures of a girl, Martha. She is a college student in New Jersey and, though she is not his girl friend, he fantasizes that she is. At the close of each day he would wash his hands and tenderly reread the letters. All the men carried necessities, knives, weapons, supplies, lighters. Others carried things more peculiar to their personalities: Bibles, condoms, comic books, dope. Everyone carried photographs. On this particular mission, to destroy a series of Viet Cong tunnels, they each carried four pounds of high explosives. One man was to go inside the tunnels while the others stood watch outside. The men wait. After a while, Lieutenant Cross, peers into the hole, concerned about the man inside. His mind wanders to thoughts of Martha. Eventually, the man emerges from the tunnel, alive. The men rejoice, but as they do, Lavender, whose prize possession was six ounces of high grade marijuana is shot down by a single gunshot.

O'Brien then offers another summary of the various possessions carried: physical objects like insecticide and religious tokens, but also various parasites and diseases. They pursue their missions with little sense of purpose, taking one step after another while bearing a range of emotions and memories.

They also discarded things, supplies, inhibitions, emotions, love, and their humanity. After Lavender's death, the men destroy the local village. Lieutenant Cross tries to avoid tears while he savagely digs a hole into the ground. He feels that his dedication to Martha had cost Lavender's life. The next day he burns Martha's letters. He resolves to be a better leader. He reminds himself that he must lead, not love, his men. He would discard love. O'Brien's stories features techniques from many war stories in previous years. Though clearly set in the Vietnam era, the repetition of the patrols resonates with the accounts of trench warfare in the Great War. Corson's and Cross's platoons walk on mindlessly, their brains in their feet, just like Downey's Private Meadows in World War II.

And like the other Vietnam stories, it accentuates the hopelessness of the situation with references to open drug use among the troops.

Vietnam is again the subject of Thom Jones' "The Pugilist at Rest" (1992; *New Yorker*, 1991). The story is cast as a reflection of a marine veteran as he looks through his Marine Corps souvenirs. He recalls the brutality of boot camp and how he was a "true believer," unlike his buddy, Jorgeson, who didn't seem to think "loving the American flag and defending democratic ideals in Southeast Asia were all that important."[30] Jorgeson aspired to be a beatnik artist in SoHo. The narrator, on the other hand, was deeply moved by a speech from the DI, Sergeant Wright:

> "You men are going off to war, and its not a pretty thing," etc. & etc., "and if Luke the Gook knocks down one of your buddies, a fellow Marine, you are going to risk your life and go in and get that Marine and you are going to bring him out. Not because I said so. No! You are going after that Marine because you_are a Marine, a member of the most elite fighting force in the world, and that man out there who's gone down is a Marine, and he's your *buddy*. He is your brother! Once you are a Marine, you are *always* a Marine and you will never let another Marine down." Etc. & etc.[31]

In spite of Jorgeson's non enthusiastic attitude, the narrator sees he is a good marine. The two cover for each other. One day, during a run on the parade ground, another man, known as "Hey Baby," shoves Jorgeson with the butt of his rifle. Our narrator smacks Hey Baby in the temple with butt of his own rifle, cracking his skull. In spite of the fact that several other men saw the incident, no one reports it to the Criminal Investigation Unit when questioned.

As part of his reverie, the narrator looks at his medals, the Navy Cross and two Silver Stars, and his airborne wings. Airborne had been Jorgeson's idea. Somehow, after basic, Joregeson had become a believer. Three days after arriving "in country" Jorgeson and the narrator were airdropped for a "routine reconnaissance patrol" in Quang Tri province. They come under attack almost immediately. Our narrator is blinded by red dirt blown in an explosion from an ant hill. His rifle is also jammed. Meanwhile, Jorgeson and the Lieutenant, Milton, are the only Americans returning fire. Milton continues to fire his .45, even after having his arm blown off. Jorgeson, singlehandedly, killed a large number of the enemy. He looks over at the narrator, still struggling to clean his rifle, and smiles. At that moment he saw an enemy "rocket grenade explode through Jorgeson's upper abdomen."[32] Our narrator is saved when two F-4s come in with explosives and napalm.

The writer then reflects on the Roman gladiator, Theogenes, and the Roman statue of "The Pugilist at Rest." The Pugilist, tired and battle scarred, is an image that resonates deeply with our narrator. He reveals that he "cut and ran from that field in Southeast Asia."[33] Eventually, after learning that he "was something quite different other than that which I had known myself to be," he drew on the "reservoir of malice, poison, and vicious sadism in my soul, and it poured forth freely in the jungles and rice paddies of Vietnam." He survived three tours of duty: "I committed unspeakable crimes and got medals for it."[34]

Having survived Vietnam, our narrator becomes brain damaged in a boxing match at Camp Pendleton. The injury leaves him with a damaged left-temporal-lobe and a type of epilepsy named after Dostoyevski. Sufferers of the malady, which many think also include St. Paul, Muhammad, Black Elk, and Joan of Arc, experience flashes of "brain lightening" that allow them to see clearly through the world's follies. Our Pugilist's glimpses of truth come at great cost, however. He wears a boxing helmet at all times to protect him from falls during seizures. A pair of dogs are his constant companions. They are trained to watch him as he sleeps, lest he suffer a seizure and suffocate in his bedclothes. His sister has introduced him to a neurosurgeon who thinks he can stop the seizures by cauterizing a spot on his brain. The procedure is called a cingulotomy. It is not a lobotomy.

He has decided to undergo the operation. He prepares by trying to get his thoughts in order. He thinks about Jorgenson, whom he wished had become an artist. He reveals his greatest sin, as a Marine: "If I had a more conventional sense of morality I would shitcan those dress blues, and I'd send that Navy Cross to Jorgeson's brother. Jorgeson was the one who pulled the John Wayne number up there near Khe Sanh, and saved my life, although I lied and took the credit for all those dead N.V.A." He thinks of Hey Baby. Maybe he should apologize to him, but he has learned from his seizures that :

> Good and Evil are only illusions. Still, I cannot help but wonder sometimes if my vision of the Supreme Reality was any more real than the demons visited upon schizophrenics and madmen. Has it all been just a stupid neurochemical event? Is there no God at all? The human heart rebels against this.[35]

Jones' Pugilist opts to accept the surgery that will take away his flashes of truth. In contrast, Bowen's Carson ("A Matter of Price") chose to live with his constant reminder. Truth was all too dangerous for the Vietnam veteran.

Twenty years after the fighting stopped in Vietnam, Robert Olen Butler's "Salem" (1994; *Mississippi Review*, 1993) looks at the war from a Vietnamese perspective. The story is a poignant companion to O'Brien's "Things They Carried," A former Vietcong soldier sits in his home pondering the news of his country's decision to repair relations with the United States, particularly to help in locating the remains of missing soldiers. He has "always been obedient to his true leaders." He went into the jungle and killed at their command, but now he feels resistant. He had lost his "manhood . . . beneath the bellow of fire from the B-52s."[36] He worries that his leaders will betray his country and turn them into Japanese. He thinks it absurd that soon "The young V.C. and U. S. soldier" will be "reborn as middle-aged friends doing business together, creating soda cans and cigarettes."[37]

He considers a package in his hands, "a twenty-four-year-old pack of Salem cigarettes" and a small photograph, the only remnants of an American he had killed with a grenade made from a Coca-Cola can. He recalls the incident:

> I could have shot him but I had made this thing and I saw him in the clearing, coming in slow but noisy, and he was nervous, he was separated and lost and I had plenty of time and I lobbed the can and it landed softly at his feet and he looked down and stared at it as if it was a gift from his American gods, as if he was thinking to pick up this Coca-Cola and drink and refresh himself.[38]

After killing the man, a routine act for him, he went through the man's possessions, looking for documents of military value. All he found was the package of cigarettes. Salem was the brand favored by "the dear father of Vietnam, Ho Chi Minh."[39] Later, in the jungle, he tries one of the Salems and is startled by the rush of menthol. He wonders if he is not being stirred by Ho's spirit. He examines the package more carefully and discovers a photograph of a young woman, tucked neatly behind the pack's cellophane.

Now, twenty-four-years later, he again ponders the pack of Salems. He understands that the soldier kept the cigarettes there so that he could see the young woman's face every time he stopped for a break, for a smoke. The realization was surprising to him: "A sentimental gesture like that from an American soldier who has come across an ocean to do the imperialist work of his country? Perhaps that is why I kept the pack of cigarettes. I am baffled by such an act from this man."[40] He realizes now that his thinking was confused, that the photo was a picture of a living human being. He remembers that in the package was a half-smoked cigarette, kept no doubt by a poor man, like himself. He believes that the man must have been a poor farmer. He realizes that he must turn the photograph in to the authorities because objects can be very important. He thinks about his country's flag, the face of Ho Chi Minh, and the fact that Ho smoked Salems:

> I turn the pack of Salem over and there is something to understand here. The two bands of color, top and bottom, are color like I sometimes have seen on the South China Sea . . . . And the sea is parted here and held within is a band of pure white and this word *Salem*, and now at last I can see clearly—how thin the line is between ignorance and wisdom—I understand all at once that there is a secret space in the word, not *Salem* but *sa* and *lem*, Vietnamese words, the one meaning fall and the other to blur, and this is the moment that I brought to the man who that very morning looked into the face of his wife and smoked and then they had to move on . . . and I was sent by my own government to sit in a tree and watch him move beneath me, frightened, and I brought him to that moment of falling and blurring.[41]

He withdraws one of the cigarettes, lights it and smokes it, again feeling the ghostly chill. He knows that the man's wife will "go to a place and she will look through many pictures and she will at last see her own face and then she will know what she must know."[42] He will keep the cigarettes, however, and one day, when he knows it is the right time, will smoke another.

After a series of grim stories about Vietnam, Butler's story ends the Vietnam section of this survey with a simple act of reconciliation. The nameless Vietnamese man puts aside his previous training, prejudice, and hatred, and resolves to perform the simple gesture of returning the photograph. The cigarette he smokes is an act of communion between himself, Ho Chi Minh, the dead man, the dead man's wife, Vietnam, and America.

Though Vietnam is laid to rest in 1994, the Civil War, or rather, the War Between the States, returns in 2004 in R. T. Smith's "The Docent" (*Missouri Review*, 2003). This delightful story is cast as a monologue by Miss Sibby, a docent at the tomb of Robert E. Lee, on the campus of Washington and Lee University. Miss Sibby's monologue is a glorious and romantic account of the life of General Lee, told from the perspective of an aging daughter of the Confederacy. Though the story is charming in its unreconstructed southernness, it emphasizes that well into the twenty-first century, division from the American Civil War, fought 140 years ago, remain with us still.

Tobias Wolff's "Awaiting Orders" (2006; *New Yorker*, 25 July 2005) is the first story in the series to address the war in Iraq. It also returns to the issue of gays in the military. Sergeant Owen Morse, a twenty-year veteran, is serving night duty in the orderly room when he takes a call from a woman asking for Specialist Billy Hart. Hart, she is told, was shipped out to Iraq the week before. After the call, Morse thinks about Hart. Although he really didn't know Hart, the young man had caught his eye. Morse felt that Hart, in another time and place, might have been a man worth pursuing. Morse, it is now revealed, is gay. He had served his twenty years on the edge of discovery. He had had an affair with a Cuban waiter who threatened to blackmail him when he broke off their relationship. He had gotten involved with a lieutenant in Iraq, but had been able to terminate the relationship when the man had been sent home with an injury. Now he was in a relationship with another NCO, who lived off post.

Later the same night, Morse receives a second call from the woman, who turns out to be Hart's sister. Morse senses that the woman is in some trouble and meets her at a restaurant after midnight. The woman, Julianne, is with a small boy, Charlie, who turns out to be Hart's son and abandoned by his drug-addicted mother. Morse is quite surprised by the revelation. While suppressing his disappointment in Hart's sexual orientation, Morse also spies men from his unit eating at a table across the restaurant. He engages the men with eye contact which is mutually acknowledged and thinks that is a good thing for him to be seen in public with a woman and a child. At the same time he feels bitter that he has to think about things that way. Julianne refuses Morse's gesture to pay for their meal, nor will she allow him to pay for a hotel room. He leaves Julianne and Charlie, knowing that they will sleep the night in her truck.

Morse tells the story to his lover, Dixon, in Dixon's townhouse. Dixon tells him that he should have invited Julianne and Charlie to stay at their home. Morse replies that he never thought of it, but he thinks differently. The presence of others in their home would destroy his domestic routine, but it would also endanger his cover. More significant, however, is his perception that the woman would be aware of the way Dixon gazed at him as a lover and how he did share the gaze in return.

Wolfe's story is remarkable not so much in his mention of the war, nor in the mention of Morse's homosexuality. Rather, the interesting thing about the story is its ordinariness. Morse is a soldier, a gay man, a human being concerned about other human beings, and yet a person who cannot sustain relationships. Again, this story utilizes depiction of what could be a somewhat unusual situation, to portray it as yet another tile in the American mosaic.

The Iraq War finally gets full treatment in Benjamin Percy's "Refresh, Refresh" (2006; *Paris Review*, Autumn/Winter 2005). The story is set in the fictional town of Crow, Oregon, high in the dessert foothills of the Cascades, and told from the perspective of an eighteen year old boy, Josh. There is not much to say about Crow, except that it is the home base of the Second Battalion of the Thirty-fourth Marines. The area around Crow had become especially valuable to the Marines lately because the terrain resembles that in Afghanistan and northern Iraq. Most of the men in town had enlisted in the Marine reserves years ago for "beer pay" in exchange for a weekend a month and two weeks in the summer. Now, however, the entire battalion had been sent to Iraq, leaving a great void in the small town:

> Our fathers—our coaches, our teachers, our barbers, our cooks, our gas station attendants and UPS deliverymen and deputies and firemen and mechanics—our fathers, so many of them, climbed onto the olive green school buses and pressed their palms to the windows and gave us the bravest and most hopeful smiles you can imagine and vanished. Just like that.[43]

Josh and his friend, Gordon, spend much of their time punching out their frustrations on each other with boxing gloves. They spend a great deal of time around a meteor crater, called "Hole in the Ground." Josh's father emails him frequently in his first days away from home, but the emails are now few and far between: "Sometimes, on the computer, I would hit refresh, refresh, *refresh*, hoping" for another message."[44] The boys are "haunted" by the absence of their fathers. Gordon and Josh fight and drink so much that their wounds never heal and their bodies age prematurely. The same is true of their fellow townspeople: "Black bags grew beneath the eyes of the sons and daughters and wives of Crow, their shoulders stooped, wrinkles enclosing their mouths like parentheses."[45]

The only men left in town are the old, the infirm, and the incapable: "Men who rarely shaved and watched daytime television in their once white underpants." Another of the men left behind was Dave Lightner, a "vulturous man" who scavenged what the fathers left behind—their wives and their sons.[46] He was the local Marine Corps recruiter. Lightner was also the Marine sent to homes to inform families when their Marine had been killed. When Lightner had told one of their football teammates that his father had been killed, the son punched him in the nose. Now, on a winter's day not long after, Lightner was standing on Josh's porch. Josh and Gordon pummel the man severely and tie him to a sled with duck tape. They haul him behind their motorcycles to the edge of the snow covered Hole in the Ground. They leave the man sobbing and the sled teetering on the edge of the crater. Then they drive to the Marine Recruiting Office, "where we would at last answer the fierce alarm of war and put our pens to paper and make our fathers proud."[47]

Percy's story presents the impact of the Iraq War in an almost allegorical form, invoking the parentless boys of *Lord of the Flies* and, more germane to this study, the village depicted in Kemble's "The Strange-Looking Man," first published in 1916. Kemble's story presented the insanity of the Great War in the scene of a German village whose only living males are severely maimed and disfigured. Percy invites the same comparison in his depiction of a town denuded of its mature, functional men.

The post-war stories portray dramatic divisions between Americans in regard to race and ethnicity. Though the awareness of racial and ethnic division is quite explicit, there is no feeling that those divisions can be overcome. Rather, one gets a feeling that we are inexplicably caught up in a situation from which there is no escape. Things aren't quite what they should be and we don't necessarily see a way out. Again, emphasis seems to be placed on the scene.

War is treated more as a constant and less as an aberration. War happens and people get hurt in war. The spiritual tone in both "Pugilist at Rest" and "Salem" shows some promise of spiritual motivation. Similar to some of the stories written after the Great War, the characters in both stories seek solace and explanation in the spiritual realm. Spirituality is used as a means of Reconciliation.

The variety of smaller military actions, particularly since the 1980s have been ignored. The writers seem to present an America far more comfortable with military action than in earlier generations. Perhaps they are so accustomed to it that they no longer feel the need to comment. Or, it is something that no longer concerns the editors.

Again, scenic portrayals seem to dominate the narrative, with a couple of interesting exceptions. Bowen's Carson ("A Matter of Price") clearly acts to make a choice in regard to a possible lobotomy and to live. Likewise, Jones' Pugilist acknowledges his responsibility in regard to his actions, but ultimately chooses an operation that will block his pain. Some mystical elements also return. Gerald's Blake and Dickerson's Chico lose their lives in a mystical sense of human sacrifice. Jones' Pugilist is portrayed in a mystical sense, one who has visions not unlike those of historical prophets. Butler's Vietnamese soldier reacts in a mystical way with the cigarette package to make the choice to return the photograph. The writers present us with a view of America that we can take or leave. For better or ill, however, we have been conditioned to accept it.

# Notes

1. John Bell Clayton, "Visitor From Philadelphia," in Martha Foley, ed., *Best American Short Stories, 1948, and Yearbook of the American Short Story* (Boston: Houghton Mifflin, 1948) 75.
2. Clayton 76.
3. George P. Elliot, "The NRACP," in Martha Foley, ed., *Best American Short Stories, 1950, and Yearbook of the American Short Story* (Boston: Houghton Mifflin, 1950) 141.
4. Elliot 142.
5. Robert O. Bowen, "A Matter of Price," in Martha Foley, ed., *Best American Short Stories, 1955, and Yearbook of the American Short Story* (Boston: Houghton Mifflin, 1955) 2.
6. Bowen 10.
7. Bowen 11.
8. Bowen 12.
9. Philip Garrigan, "Fly, Fly, Little Dove," in Martha Foley, ed., *Best American Short Stories, 1947, and Yearbook of the American Short Story* (Boston: Houghton Mifflin, 1947) 100.
10. Garrigan 102-03.
11. Garrigan 104.
12. John Bar Gerald, "Walking Wounded," in Martha Foley and David Burnett, eds., *Best American Short Stories, 1969 and Yearbook of the American Short Story.* (New York: Ballantine, 1969) 38.
13. Gerald, "Walking," 39.
14. Gerald, "Walking," 42-43.
15 Gerald, "Walking," 46.
16. Gerald, "Walking," 47.
17. Gerald, "Walking," 48.
18. Gerald, "Blood Letting," in Martha Foley and David Burnett, eds. *Best American Short Stories, 1970 and Yearbook of the American Short Story* (New York: Ballantine, 1970) 128.
19. Gerald, "Blood," 125.
20. Gerald, "Blood," 127.
21. Gerald, "Blood," 129.
22. Gerald, "Blood," 130.
23. Gerald, "Blood," 131.
24. Larry Heinemann, "The First Clean Fact," in Stanley Elkin, with Shannon Ravenel, eds., *The Best American Short Stories, 1980, Selected from U. S. and Canadian Magazines, including the Yearbook of the American Short Story* (Boston: Houghton Mifflin, 1980) 217.
25. Heinemann 217.
26. Heinemann 218.
27. Heinemann 219.

28. Heinemann  220.

29. Heinemann  220.

24. Thom Jones, "The Pugilist at Rest," in Robert Stone, with Katrina Kennison, eds., *The Best American Short Stories, 1992, Selected from U. S. and Canadian Magazines, including the Yearbook of the American Short Story* (Boston: Houghton Mifflin, 1992) 122.

25. Jones 122.

26. Jones 130.

27. Jones 133.

28. Jones 134.

29. Jones 139.

30. Robert Olen Butler, "Salem,"in Tobias Wolff, with Katrina Kennison, eds., *The Best American Short Stories, 1994, Selected from U. S. and Canadian Magazines, including the Yearbook of the American Short Story* (Boston: Houghton Mifflin, 1994)  27.

31. Butler 28.

32. Butler 26.

33. Butler 27.

34. Butler 30.

35. Butler 33.

36. Butler 33.

37. Benjamin Percy, "Refresh, Refresh," in Ann Patchett, with Katrina Kennison, eds., *The Best American Short Stories, 2006, Selected from U. S. and Canadian Magazines, including the Yearbook of the American Short Story* (Boston: Houghton Mifflin, 2006) 92.

38. Percy 94.

39. Percy 101.

40. Percy 95-96.

41. Percy 104.

# Conclusion: Falling Into America

Over the course of this study we have encountered a variety of characters and situations, each affected by war and the military. We've seen men caught in the devastating trench warfare of the Great War, where the carnage was so awful that it sent a generation seeking closure in the spiritual world. We have heard the women of World War Two give their testimony on the effect of war on the home front through the relationship with their husbands, lovers, sons, and brothers. We've read about the displaced and the despondent, the broken and the battered. In spite of it all, each person has done their part and has fallen into America. The ex-soldiers persevere. The restless spirits find a resting place. Families heal, reform, and reconstitute themselves. The women endure.

Young Jack Fuller, hampered by a dissipated, tragic youth, reforms and regroups to fall into America. Loeb, the Jewish refugee from Nazi Germany, falls into America. Dreher, the would-be Austrian scriptwriter falls and stumbles into America. Brownlea, the leftist member of a bomber crew, puts his life on the line and eventually loses it for America. Blake, the Air Force reservist, conflicted by just about every aspect of his life, takes his life for America. Even the nameless former Viet Cong soldier, who finds so much meaning in a pack of Salem cigarettes, falls into America.

The America, and the world depicted through American lenses, is far from perfect. There is dysfunction, racism, and anti-Semitism. It is a nation affected by a military that tests, if not conquers, the human spirit. The response to these varying circumstances, however, is not despair. The characters trudge on. There is always some vestige of hope.

Bob, the hard-bitten brother in "My Brother's Second Funeral," perhaps one of the more cynical characters in this study, is still optimistic. He cannot believe that his brother gave his life for some higher cause. He cannot pray: "Sometimes I'd like to, but I don't know how." Clearly, he is a broken man, but he does not dismiss the hope that he can heal. As Marek says in Gellhorn's "Weekend at

Grimsby," a person cannot live if they are obsessed with the past. In all these stories we see people trying to find a way to move on.

The rhetorical nature of these stories changes over time. The stories of the Great War seem heavy handed, with shifts in narration and structure. By World War II narrative devices are much more subtle, though some stories, particularly Shaw's, feature an oratorical bent. With the stories of World War II, however, also comes a stronger enthymematic touch. The stories seem to connect with a set of experiences broadly felt. Their touches of realism allow some dissension about the war to be expressed, not through speech, but depiction. In essence, the facts of the story speak for themselves. The post-war stories, particularly the ones set in training camp, appear less subtle.

There is a preachy quality about the post-war stories that demands more explicit attention. Without the exigency of a declared, ongoing war, writers needed to be more explicit. The context of the Vietnam War was so explicit, with daily body counts, battle scenes, and antiwar demonstrations on the nightly news, writers again resort to much more heavy handed narration in their stories. Heinemann's "The First Clean Fact" even goes back to the device of the story-teller, though in the end we learn that this one is dead. The Vietnam stories also return to a degree of spirituality in "The Pugilist at Rest," "Blood Letting," and "Salem." It stands to reason that some of the hopelessness felt in the inconclusive aftermath of Vietnam would resonate with that felt after the Great War.

The pentadic analysis may be the most revealing aspect. The mythology of the United States has long rested on narratives about men and women leading the country toward its God-given purpose. Indeed, much work has been done over the last 35 years to include women and other underrepresented groups in those narratives. American heroes overcome the land, the elements, and outmoded ways of thinking to craft a new nation. We get vestiges of that myth in many of the stories we have reviewed from the Civil War and in many of the stories written at the time the United States entered the Great War. Beyond that point, however, the stories reviewed here present a different American ethos, one which is determined more by the conditions around them than by the sheer force and will of great persons. Our soldiers from World War II are caught up in a world over which they have no control. They simply fall in step behind the men in front of them and react. Of the soldiers portrayed from World War II, only Crispin makes a heroic choice. It is no wonder, then, that General George C. Marshall had to ask Frank Capra to create a film series telling the soldiers "Why We Fight." The stories of the post war years treated important topics like race and civil rights, and while those accounts feature some heroes (like Blasingame's Lt. Henderson), many other characters stand on the periphery, or play the "old army game." The post world war stories portray the agents as mundane elements of a scene that is destined to move towards inevitable consequences, independent of individual actions.

It could be that the emphasis on science and social science in the 20th century led to a conditioning of the American mind that saw things in objective, scientific terms. As we saw that conditions like poverty and prejudice led to societal malfunction, could it be that we were co-opted to view all things in those terms? The role of the agent in these stories is strongly diminished. Virtually all characters are swept up in the overwhelming influence of the scene.

The stories concerning the twentieth century wars do not emphasize the agent. Peculiarly, however, the eight Civil War stories written during the period of 1915-2004 all focus on agents, revealing an idealistic perspective. One would not think that American idealism is lost in the twentieth century, but if we judged its existence solely on the basis of these short stories, it would certainly appear to have been lost. Not only did the Civil War preserve the Union (a point that the stories emphasize over the elimination of slavery), but it also seems to define the nation's ideals in a static context. The civil war stories are clearly nostalgic yearnings for what was perceived as a more noble time. It is interesting to note that the stories of the Great War and World War II are now over 60 and 80 years old. The Civil War had been over for only 50 years when the first stories written about it in *Best American Short Stories* appeared. Why haven't the twentieth century wars been the subject of such nostalgia in short stories? The stories of the Civil War take us back to an idealistic time, while subsequent stories do not.

Rhetorically, the short story is rather versatile. Though fiction can creep into the consciousness of the reader stealthily, in the guise of a story, it can also be quite overt. The short story can be expressed in quite lifelike terms, but also as an allegory, or fable. It may provide a very large amount of context and, conversely, very little.

In the case of the stories from the Great War, the nature of the stories changes according to a shifting context. The stories of World War II resonate with a variety of subtle contexts. They do not speak in opposition to the war, but they engage their reader in a sort of shared discomfort. The post-war writings are brash, as if the writers are proclaiming epiphanies they feel are unnoticed by those around them. Each, however, delivers a fairly clear message.

Martha Foley brought something of a feminist perspective to her selection of stories. The attention to women's lives, roles, and feelings provides a different view of the Second World War than in the first. Her editions of *Best American Short Stories* present to the reader previously unseen impacts of war. Stories about and written by women dominate the stories published during the war. Nonetheless, the masculine gaze dominates the stories addressed in the post-war period, including those selected by Foley. Interestingly, none of the more contemporary stories feature any inclusion of the now integrated role women play in the military. Anticipating contemporary trends, Foley's volumes did feature two stories touching on the issue of gays in the military, a theme untouched until the most recent volumes.

I remarked in regard to Chapter One that the stories of the Great War still bear the oral imprint of the storyteller. The stories from that point afterward, however, bear not so much the stamp of a writer as they bear the mark of the painter. Rhetorical depiction, word pictures that present a feeling in time and place, may well be more powerful than arguments. They present a situation in a seemingly objective fashion, but without comment. Just as Goya or Caravaggio utilized texture, light, and shadowing to highlight the various aspects of humanity, so do our writers utilize words. The intentions of the rhetor are masked, to the extent that there is an overt intention. The images they present, however, are quite powerful.

It should come as no surprise that the short story can be seen as a powerful rhetorical force. Homer's epic tales, the Iliad and Odyssey, the forebears of so many stories, were passed down via an oral tradition and are chocked full of the stuff that comprises classical rhetorical theory. Like the Homeric epics, the stories reviewed here rely on word pictures, depictions, that are, in essence, epic similes. By painting word pictures, Homer, the blind bard, brought his stories to life. Likewise, our contemporary authors have used rhetorical depiction to bring life to situations that had been too far reduced by mere words.

The images presented serve to undercut the sterilization of the situations which have been neutralized by political and diplomatic terms. I cannot speak with authority on the reactions of previous generations, but I can attest to the vivid contrast brought by the stories on Vietnam in contrast to discussions of "peace with honor" and "vietnamization." It is very difficult to read the Vietnam stories and remain convinced that peace could be brought with anything resembling honor.

Short fiction is clearly a barometer of the moods and attitudes of the American public. Those moods and attitudes, however, are not always articulated in other public records of the time. Through the indirect form of rhetorical depiction, the short story can portray events in ways that connect the hearts, minds, indeed souls, of writers and readers in unspoken ways. It is a connection, in Foley's words, "like an act of love."

# Bibliography

Aristotle. *Aristotle on Rhetoric: A Theory of Civic Discourse; Newly Translated with Introduction, Notes, and Appendixes by George A. Kennedy.* Oxford: Oxford University Press, 1991.

Baum, Vicki. "This Healthy Life." In Foley, *1943*, 1-9.

Beattie, Ann, with Shannon Ravenel, eds. *The Best American Short Stories, 1987, Selected from U. S. and Canadian Magazines.* Boston: Houghton Mifflin, 1987.

Beck, Warren. "Boundary Line." In Foley, *1943*, 10-22.

Bellow, Saul. "Notes of a Dangling Man." In Foley, *1944*, 21-40.

Bitzer, Lloyd. "Aristotle's Enthymeme Revisited." *Quarterly Journal of Speech* 45 (1959): 399-408.

Black, Edwin. *Rhetorical Criticism: A Study in Method.* 1965; University of Wisconsin Press, 1978.

Blasingame, Wyatt. "Man's Courage." In Foley, *1957*, 32-38.

Bowen, Robert O. "A Matter of Price." In Foley, *1955*, 1-12.

Boyle, Kay. "Anschluss." In O'Brien, *1940*, 1-19.

Boyle, Kay. "The Lost." In Foley, *1952*, 31-48.

Breuer, Bessie. "Bury Your Own Dead." In Foley, *1946*, 56-73.

Broderick, Francis L. "Return by Faith." In Foley, *1947*, 1-16.

Brokaw, Tom. *The Greatest Generation.* New York: Dell, 2001.

Buckner, Robert. "The Man Who Won the War." In O'Brien, 1937, 1-14.

Burke, Kenneth. *A Grammar of Motives.* 1945; Berkeley, CA: University of California Press, 1969.

Burnett, Dana. "Beyond the Cross." In O'Brien, *1923*, 98-142.

Burt, Maxwell Struthers. "The Blood-Red One." In O'Brien, *1919*, 96-107.

Butler, Robert Olen. "Salem." In Wolff, *1994*, 26-33.

Canfield, Dorothy. "The Knot Hole." In Foley, *1944*, 41-61.

Clayton, John Bell. "Visitor From Philadelphia." In Foley, *1948*, 73-77.

Cobb, Irvin S., "No Dam' Yankee." In O'Brien, *1928*, 94-112.

Comfort, Will Levington. "Chautonville." In O'Brien, *1915*, 46-54.

Critchell, Lawrence (Lt.). "Flesh and Blood." In Foley, *1946*, 128-146.

DeJong, David Cornell. "That Frozen Hour." In Foley, *1942*, 75-92.

De Pereda, Prudencio. "The Spaniard." In O'Brien, *1938*, 208-217.

Dickerson, George. "Chico." In Foley, *1963*, 116-131.

Downey, Harris. "The Hunters." In Foley, *1951*, 100-14.

Downey, Harris. "Crispin's Way." In Foley, *1953*, 101-111.

Drake, Albert. "The Chicken Which Became a Rat." In Foley, *1971*, 86-106.

Dubus, Andre. "Cadence." In Foley, *1975*, 80-99.

Dwiggins, W. A. "La Derniére Mobilisation." In O'Brien, *1915*, 55-56.

Elkin, Stanley, with Shannon Ravenel, eds. *The Best American Short Stories, 1980, Selected from U. S. and Canadian Magazines, including the Yearbook of the American Short Story*. Boston: Houghton Mifflin, 1980.

Elliott, George P. "The NRACP." In Foley, *1950*, 109-142.

Fenton, Edward. "Burial in the Desert." In Foley, *1945*, 49-63.

Fleming, Berry. "Strike Up the Stirring Music." In Foley, *1944*, 117-124.

Foley, Martha, ed. *Best American Short Stories, 1942, and Yearbook of the American Short Story*. Boston: Houghton Mifflin, 1942.

Foley, Martha, ed. *Best American Short Stories, 1943, and Yearbook of the American Short Story*. Boston: Houghton Mifflin, 1943.

Foley, Martha, ed. *Best American Short Stories, 1944, and Yearbook of the American Short Story*. Boston: Houghton Mifflin, 1944.

Foley, Martha, ed. *Best American Short Stories, 1945, and Yearbook of the American Short Story*. Boston: Houghton Mifflin, 1945.

Foley, Martha, ed. *Best American Short Stories, 1946, and Yearbook of the American Short Story*. Boston: Houghton Mifflin, 1946.

Foley, Martha, ed. *Best American Short Stories, 1947, and Yearbook of the American Short Story*. Boston: Houghton Mifflin, 1947.

Foley, Martha, ed. *Best American Short Stories, 1948, and Yearbook of the American Short Story*. Boston: Houghton Mifflin, 1948.

Foley, Martha, ed. *Best American Short Stories, 1949, and Yearbook of the American Short Story*. Boston: Houghton Mifflin, 1949.

Foley, Martha, ed. *Best American Short Stories, 1950, and Yearbook of the American Short Story*. Boston: Houghton Mifflin, 1950.

Foley, Martha, ed. *Best American Short Stories, 1951, and Yearbook of the American Short Story*. Boston: Houghton Mifflin, 1951.

Foley, Martha, ed. *Best American Short Stories, 1952, and Yearbook of the American Short Story*. Boston: Houghton Mifflin, 1952.

Foley, Martha, ed. *Best American Short Stories, 1953, and Yearbook of the American Short Story*. Boston: Houghton Mifflin, 1953.

Foley, Martha, ed. *Best American Short Stories, 1954, and Yearbook of the American Short Story*. Boston: Houghton Mifflin, 1954.

Foley, Martha, ed. *Best American Short Stories, 1955, and Yearbook of the American Short Story*. Boston: Houghton Mifflin, 1955.

Foley, Martha, ed. *Best American Short Stories, 1956, and Yearbook of the American Short Story*. New York: Ballantine, 1956.

Foley, Martha, ed. *Best American Short Stories, 1957, and Yearbook of the American Short Story*. Boston: Houghton Mifflin, 1957

Foley, Martha, ed. *Best American Short Stories, 1958, and Yearbook of the American Short Story*. Boston: Houghton Mifflin, 1958.

Foley, Martha, ed. *Best American Short Stories, 1959 and Yearbook of the American Short Story*. Boston: Houghton Mifflin, 1959

Foley, Martha, ed. *Best American Short Stories, 1960, and Yearbook of the American Short Story*. New York: Ballantine, 1960.

Foley, Martha, ed. *Best American Short Stories, 1961, and Yearbook of the American Short Story*. New York: Ballantine, 1961.

Foley, Martha and David Burnett, eds. *Best American Short Stories, 1962, and Yearbook of the American Short Story*. New York: Ballantine, 1962.

Foley, Martha and David Burnett, eds. *Best American Short Stories, 1963, and Yearbook of the American Short Story*. New York: Ballantine, 1963.

Foley, Martha and David Burnett, eds. *Best American Short Stories, 1966, and Yearbook of the American Short Story*. New York: Ballantine, 1966.

Foley, Martha and David Burnett, eds. *Best American Short Stories, 1968, and Yearbook of the American Short Story*. New York: Ballantine, 1968.

Foley, Martha and David Burnett, eds. *Best American Short Stories, 1969 and Yearbook of the American Short Story*. New York: Ballantine, 1969.

Foley, Martha, and David Burnett, eds. *Best American Short Stories, 1970, and Yearbook of the American Short Story*. New York: Ballantine, 1970.

Foley, Martha, and David Burnett, eds. *Best American Short Stories, 1971, and Yearbook of the American Short Story*. Boston: Houghton Mifflin, 1971.

Foley, Martha, ed. *Best American Short Stories, 1973, and Yearbook of the American Short Story*. Boston: Houghton Mifflin, 1973.

Foley, Martha, ed. *Best American Short Stories, 1975, and Yearbook of the American Short Story*. Boston: Houghton Mifflin, 1975.

Foley, Martha, ed. *Best American Short Stories, 1976, and Yearbook of the American Short Story*. Boston: Houghton Mifflin, 1976.

Foley, Martha, ed. *Best American Short Stories, 1977, and Yearbook of the American Short Story*. Boston: Houghton Mifflin, 1977.

Freedley, Mary Mitchell. "Blind Vision." In O'Brien, *1918*, 85-91.

Fussell, Paul. *The Great War and Modern Memory*. New York: Oxford University Press, 1975.

Fussell, Paul. "Writing in Wartime," in *Thank God for the Atom Bomb and Other Essays*. New York: Summit Books, 1988, 53-81.

Fussell, Paul. *Wartime: Understanding and Behavior in the Second World War*. New York: Oxford University Press, 1989.

Gardner, John, with Shannon Ravenel, eds. *The Best American Short Stories, 1982, Selected from U. S. and Canadian Magazines.* Boston: Houghton Mifflin, 1982.

Garrett, George. "The Old Army Game." In Foley, *1962*, 96-107.

Garrigan, Philip. "Fly, Fly, Little Dove." In Foley, *1947*, 99-105.

Gellhorn, Martha. "Weekend at Grimsby." In Foley, *1952*, 160-180.

Gerald, John Bart. "Walking Wounded." In Foley, *1969*, 37-48.

Gerald, John Bart. "Blood Letting." In Foley, *1970*, 125-131.

Gerry, Bill. "Understand What I Mean." In Foley, *1945*, 71-81.

Gold, Ivan. "The Nickel Misery of George Washington Carver Brown." Foley, *1961*, 92-131.

Gregory, Vahan Krikorian. "Athens, Greece, 1942." In Foley, *1953*, 145-153.

Griffith, Beatrice. "In the Flow of Time." In Foley, *1949*, 106-116.

Hahn, Emily. "It Never Happened." In Foley, *1945*, 99-108.

Hale, Nancy. "Those are as Brothers." In Foley, *1942*, 129-140.

Heinemann, Larry. "The First Clean Fact." In Elkin, *1980*, 210-220.

Hemingway, Ernest. "Under the Ridge." In O'Brien, *1940*, 109-122.

Heth, Edward Harris. "Under the Ginko Tree." In Foley, *1947*, 208-220.

Humphrey, G. "The Father's Hand." In O'Brien, *1918*, 125-30.

Johnson, Fanny Kemble. "The Strange-Looking Man." In O'Brien, *1917*, 361-364.

Johnson, Josephine. "The Rented Room." In Foley, *1944*, 141-163.

Jones, Thom, "The Pugilist at Rest." In Stone, *1992*, 121-130

Just, Ward. "Dietz at War." In Foley, *1976,* 133-144.

Jordan, Virgil. "Vengeance is Mine." In O'Brien, *1915*, 145-152.

Kenary, James S. "Going Home." In Foley, *1973*, 166-179.

Levinson, Peter J. *Tommy Dorsey: Livin' in a Great Big Way: A Biography.* Cambridge, MA: Da Capo Press, 2005.

Liebling, A. J. "Run, Run, Run, Run." In Foley, *1946*, 255-276.

Liebling, A. J. "The Foamy Fields," in *Just Enough Liebling: Classic Work by the Legendary New Yorker Writer.* New York: North Point Press, 2004, 104-148.

Litwik, Leo. E. "In Shock." In *Foley, 1968*, 221-235.

Lussu, Emilio. "Your General Does Not Sleep." In O'Brien, *1940*, 170-93.

MacMillan, Ian. "Proud Monster—Sketches." In Gardner, *1982*, 287-98.

March, William. "Fifteen From Company K." In O'Brien, *1931*, 202-213.

Marquand, J. P. "Good Morning, Major." In O'Brien, *1927*, 213-239.

McKenna, Richard. "The Sons of Martha." In Foley, *1968*, 236-256.

McLaughlin, Robert. "Poor Everybody." In Foley, *1945,* 123-132.

Moore, Lorrie, with Katrina Kenison, eds. *The Best American Short Stories, 2004, Elected from U. S. and Canadian Magazines.* Boston: Houghton Mifflin, 2004.

Moseley, Katharine Prescott. "The Story Vinton Heard at Mallorie." In O'Brien, *1918*, 191-199.

Newhouse, Edward. "My Brother's Second Funeral." In Foley, *1950*, 317-327.

O'Brien, Edward J. "Introduction." *The Best Short Stories of 1915 and the Yearbook of the American Short Story.* Ed. O'Brien. Boston: Small, Maynard and Company, 1916.

O'Brien, Edward J., ed. *The Best Short Stories of 1916 and the Yearbook of the American Short Story.* Boston: Small, Maynard and Company, 1917.

O'Brien, Edward J., ed. *The Best Short Stories of 1917 and the Yearbook of the American Short Story.* Boston: Small, Maynard and Company, 1918.

O'Brien, Edward J., ed. *The Best Short Stories of 1918 and the Yearbook of the American Short Story.* Boston: Small, Maynard and Company, 1919.

O'Brien, Edward J., ed. *The Best Short Stories of 1919 and the Yearbook of the American Short Story.* Boston: Small, Maynard and Company, 1920.

O'Brien, Edward J., ed. *The Best Short Stories of 1923 and the Yearbook of the American Short Story.* Boston: Small, Maynard and Company, 1924.

O'Brien, Edward J., ed. *The Best Short Stories of 1927 and the Yearbook of the American Short Story.* New York: Dodd, Mead and Company, 1927.

O'Brien, Edward J., ed. *The Best Short Stories of 1931 and the Yearbook of the American Short Story.* New York: Dodd, Mead and Company, 1931.

O'Brien, Edward J., ed. *The Best Short Stories of 1932 and the Yearbook of the American Short Story.* New York: Dodd, Mead and Company, 1932.

O'Brien, Edward J., ed. *The Best Short Stories of 1937 and the Yearbook of the American Short Story.* Boston: Houghton Mifflin Company, 1937.

O'Brien, Edward J., ed. *The Best Short Stories of 1938 and the Yearbook of the American Short Story.* Boston: Houghton Mifflin Company, 1938.

O'Brien, Edward J., ed. *The Best Short Stories of 1940 and the Yearbook of the American Short Story.* Boston: Houghton Mifflin Company, 1940.

O'Brien, Tim. "Going After Cacciato." In Foley, *1977*, 256-274.

O'Brien, Tim. "The Things They Carried." In Beattie, *1987*, 287-305.

O'Reilly, Mary Boyle. "In Berlin." In O'Brien, *1915*, 196.

Patchett, Ann, with Katrina Kenison, eds. *The Best American Short Stories, 2006, Selected from U. S. and Canadian Magazines.* Boston: Houghton Mifflin, 2006.

Pelley, William Dudley. "The Toast to the Forty-Five." In O'Brien, *1918*, 200-222.

Percy, Benjamin. "Refresh, Refresh." In Patchett, *2006,* 91-104.

Pfeffer, Irving. "All Prisoners Here." In Foley, *1949*, 219-237.

Poe, Edgar Allan. "On the Aim and Technique of the Short Story." In *What is the Short Story?*, rev. ed. , Eugene Current-Garcia and Walton R. Patrick, eds. Glenview, IL: Scott, Foresman, *1974*, pp. 7-18

Portugal, Ruth. "Neither Here nor There." In Foley, *1944*, 295-308.

Portugal, Ruth. "Call a Solemn Assembly." In Foley, *1945*, 170-179.

Rhodes, Harrison. "Extra Men." In O'Brien , *1918*, 223-31.

Roberts, Phyllis, 'Hero." In Foley, *1960*, 266-280.

Robbins, Tom. "The Chink and the Clock People." In Foley, *1977*, 275-290.

Rosten, Leo. "The Guy in Ward 4." In Foley, *1959*, 224-238.

Roth, Philip. "The Defender of the Faith." In Foley, *1960*, 281-307.

Salinger, J. D. "A Girl I Knew." In Foley, *1949*, 248-260.

Schulberg, Budd Wilson. "The Real Viennese Schmaltz." In Foley, *1942*, 259-268.

Shaw, Irwin. "Preach on the Dusty Roads." In Foley, *1943*, 292-300.

Shaw, Irwin. "The Veterans Reflect." In Foley, *1944*, 345-357.

Shaw, Irwin. "Gunners' Passage." In Foley, *1945*, 238-256.

Shaw, Irwin. "Act of Faith." In Foley, *1947*, 433-439.

Siegel, Jules. "In the Land of the Morning Calm, Déjà vu." In Foley, *1970*, 331-253.

Singmaster, Elsie, "The Survivors: A Memorial Day Story." In O'Brien, *1915*, 226-234.

Singmaster, Elsie "Penance." In O'Brien, *1916*, 282-293.

Smith, R. T., "The Docent." In Moore, *2004*, 376-385.

Springer, Fleta Campbell. "Solitaire." In O'Brien, *1918*, 232-57.

Stallings, Lawrence, "Gentleman in Blue." In O'Brien, *1932*, 231-242.

Stewart, Solon K. "The Contract of Corporal Twing." In O'Brien, *1923*, 322-338.

Stimson, F. J., "By Due Process of Law." In O'Brien, *1923*, 339-361.

Stone, Robert, with Katrina Kennison, eds. *The Best American Short Stories, 1992, Selected from U. S. and Canadian Magazines.* Boston: Houghton Mifflin, 1980.

Street, Julian. "The Bird of Serbia." In O'Brien, *1918*, 268-92.

Terkel, Studs. *"The Good War:" An Oral History of World War II.* New York: Pantheon, 1984.

Thielen, Benedict. "Lieutenant Pearson." In O'Brien, *1937*, 340-353.

Tüting, Bernard Johann. "The Family Chronicle." In O'Brien, *1932*, 243-252.

Updike, John and Katrina Kenison, eds. *Best American Short Stories of the Twentieth Century.* Boston: Houghton Mifflin, 2000.

Vatsek, Joan. "The Bees." In Foley, 1942, 372-384.

Wichelns, Herbert August. "The Literary Criticism of Oratory." In [A. M. Drummond, ed.] *Studies in Rhetoric and Public Speaking in Honor of James Albert Winans by Pupils and Colleagues.* New York: The Century Company, 1925, 181-216.

Whitehill, Joseph. "One Night for Several Samurai." In Foley, *1966*, 321-360.

Wolff, Tobias, with Katrina Kenison, eds. *The Best American Short Stories, Selected from U. S. and Canadian Magazines, 1994.* Boston: Houghton Mifflin, 1994.

Wolff, Tobias. "Awaiting Orders." In Patchett, *2006*, 20-29.

Wood, Frances Gilchrist. "The White Battalion." In O'Brien, *1918*, 325-332.

# Index

www.ingramcontent.com/pod-product-compliance
Lightning Source LLC
Chambersburg PA
CBHW030653110726
47901CB00002B/693